This is a work of fiction. Similarities to real people, places, or events are entirely coincidental.

HER ASSASSINS

First edition. May 15, 2018.

Written by Helene Gadot.

Dedication

For all the readers who are sick of choosing between love interests.

Acknowledgments

Thank you to the entire reverse harem community. I don't know who started it, but I have had a blast reading and writing the genre. Without you guys, this story would never have been told.

To Liz, Heather, and Alex—thank you for helping me make this book as awesome as possible.

To my husband—thank you for putting up with my crazy hours and helping me around the house.

And finally, thank you to everyone who bought, read, and spread the word about this book. You guys are the greatest.

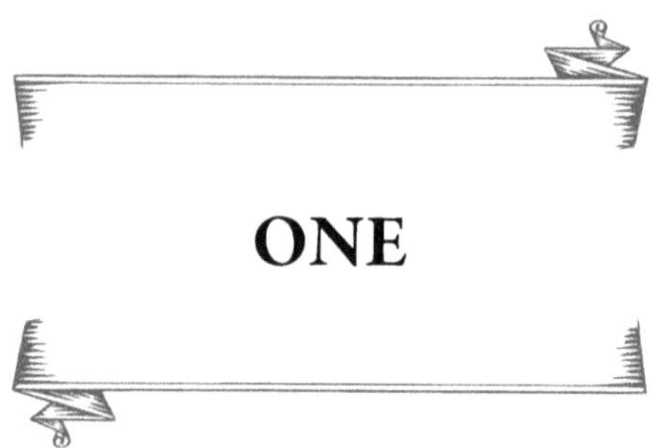

ONE

Perched on a stool in the center of the smoky tavern, my fingers plucked at the strings of my ukulele as I began my song. I sang out in protest of Faligrey's laws, against the kindred souls. My bitterness and heartbreak painted my voice with low, husky tones.

This was for my parents, for the drudge of a life they led because they dared to love each other and build a life together despite not being kindred souls. I refused to rest, to accept the life they led, the life I led. The banishments, always moving from village to village, never accepted, never making friends.

It was a lonely life, but the three of us had each other. Then the poverty got to them, bending them until they broke and the sickness took them both in the same week.

On my own ever since with nothing but my father's ukulele and a small pack of belongings, I made my way as a traveling bard, singing in taverns until my seditious lyrics got me thrown out of town.

The patrons stirred with unease as my lyrics sank in. Most listeners paid more attention to the music instead of the words. Sometimes it took a bit for it to click in their brains.

One man leaned forward from the shadows, a hood over his head like he was trying to remain hidden, but my voice drew him forward. His eyes shined like starlight and they caught me in their deep, gleaming pools.

Tearing my attention away from the mysterious man, I moved into the second song, one crooning with nostalgia and longing. My emotions rose, trying to cut off my voice, but I shoved them away. I'd release them once I was alone with the stars, not here, not now.

A small roll sailed towards me, but it fell a foot short. They hoped it would send me running away, but it wouldn't. Boos and hisses whispered from the shadows and corners of the tavern.

My songs weren't technically illegal, we were supposed to have freedom of expression, but it still made people uncomfortable and angry to hear songs against one of the strictest laws in Faligrey.

But I wanted those who never found their kindreds, those whose kindreds were a disappointment, those who lost theirs and had to spend the rest of their lives without love, those who were branded bastards to know they were not alone. That someone understood their plight, that someone saw them, that someone spoke for them, fought for them.

Sometimes it felt like I was screaming into an empty void with only the stars to hear me. But there were times. Times when desperate voices have whispered their thanks under the cover of night, the press of a grateful hand, the small gifts wrapped in cloth, the coins slipped into my hat.

It made every piece of thrown food, every bruise, every sneer, every hateful word worth it.

My third song was different. I tucked the ukulele onto my back and stood behind the stool, slamming down a beat with two tin cups onto the wooden surface. Instead of singing, I spoke the lyrics, a poem loud and angry and full of fire. My boots stomped the planks on the floor, harmonizing with the tin cups, pounding out my rage.

My voice rose over the muttering and jeers of the tavern patrons.

As I began the last stanza, a harsh hand wrapped around my upper arm. I didn't let it distract me and kept speaking my truths even as I fumbled with my cups. I managed to shove them into the pockets of my coat and I pulled my ukulele around to my chest to keep it safe from harm as they dragged me towards the door. The last words of the song fell from my lips as I was shoved outside, barely keeping my feet.

The tavern owner spit in my direction. "You're not welcome here. I suggest you get out of town before I call the royal guard on you."

I straightened my coat and shot him a crass gesture with my free hand. This was why I got my payment upfront before I performed. The few people still milling about on the darkened streets gave me curious looks, but I avoided eye contact and hurried to the edge of the village where I hid my bag of provisions. I learned the hard way years ago to not bring my things with me. It was hard enough to escape sometimes with my father's ukulele still safe in my arms.

Time to try the next village. Hopefully before word of my inflammatory songs reached them. Once I had my pack strapped over my shoulders, I walked through the night for an hour, wanting distance between my home for the night and the village. I'd had people try to follow me before to teach me a lesson.

A copse of trees and bushes arranged in a fairy ring circle would make the perfect home for the night. The leaves on the trees were thick, providing coverage. I perched on a fallen log, stretching out my sore legs in front of me while I rummaged through my pack. I pulled out my flint and one of my few remaining tins of food and the last scrap of cheese. I needed to purchase more supplies before I performed in the next village.

With a small fire crackling and keeping me company, I smiled up at the stars and raised my tin cup of warm brandy at their friendly light.

"Mama, Papa, if you're up there, I miss you. I hope you're together, finally free and happy and safe." I was convinced my whispered, broken words reached them. It was the only thing that comforted me in their absence, the thought of them reunited in death.

I drained the drink and snuggled into the blankets I had laid out on the spongy moss, using my pack as a pillow. Exhaustion plucked at me, the usual memories and worries not plaguing me on this night.

A tension in my chest, so tight it was painful, woke me up. My eyes popped open as I searched the blackness of the night for a threat.

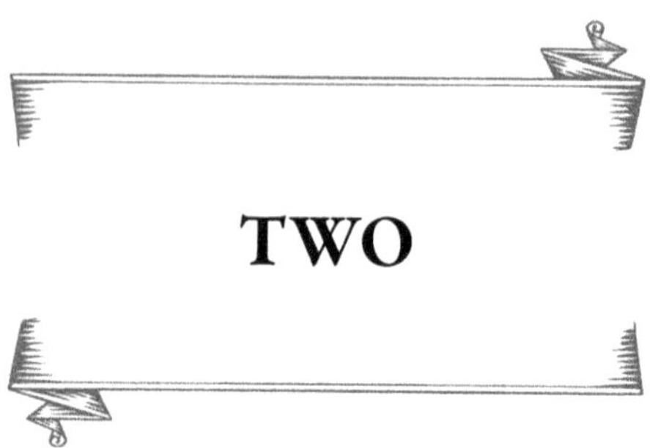

TWO

My heart thudded in my still tightening chest and the skin on the back of my neck prickled. I wasn't alone. Someone found me. I slipped my hand into my pocket and slid out my dagger. I wasn't the most skilled fighter, but it only took one lucky stab.

My chest worsened, making it hard to breathe. I didn't understand what was going on why my body was reacting this way. How I knew someone was out here.

Was I having a panic attack? Had my subconscious heard the snap of a twig and warned me? I'd felt nothing like it before. The sanctity of my camps had never been invaded. I always chose places far from traveler's paths and roads.

I kept my eyes slit, pretending I'm asleep and unaware of my uninvited and unwelcome company. Shadows grew around me even though there wasn't the slightest breeze in the air. I tightened my grip on the knife hidden beneath my blanket, my entire body trembling with tension.

Hands gripped from behind without me even realizing they were there, a palm slapping over my mouth, an arm winding around my middle, trapping my arms to my body. I thrashed against him, fighting to free myself, but his hold was strong. Two more people melt from the trees, stepping into moonlight and the waning glow of my fire. They were huge, tall and muscular and deadly.

This was not going to go well for me.

The one holding me turned me onto my back, plucking the knife from my fingers. My pulse pounded, but the tension in my chest disappeared. The pain faded away and calm swept over my body.

My brain screamed at me to fight, to move, to do something, but I was caught, lost in his eyes, eyes the color of starlight.

"What are you waiting for, Whist? Finish it." One of the other men spoke, his voice smooth and husky like the brandy I drank before bed.

The one holding me, Whist, shook his head in confusion. "I can't." It was the man from the tavern.

"Impotence at your age? You're a little young for that, aren't you?" The other man laughed and drew closer, his movements fluid until he met my eyes and stumbled, falling to his knees beside me, the humor vanishing from his face.

Whist growled at the funny man's closeness, yanking me tighter to him. "Back off, Sky. You're not touching her."

Sky's wide eyes didn't leave mine. "I'm afraid you will have to share, my friend."

Whist relaxed his hold on me the slightest bit. "You too?"

The third man, the one with the voice that echoed deep in my bones approached. "What the hell is going on?"

My brain finally forced the rest of me into action and I bucked against Whist's grip. "Let me go. What do you want from me? How did you even find me? Who are you?"

"We're here to kill you."

THREE

"What?" I struggled harder, panic making my head spin. Why they hell were they going to kill me? Who were they?

Sky shushed me and held his hands out to his sides. "We will not hurt you, doll. We can't."

The third man with the voice dropped to his knees as well beside Sky, the one who thought he was funny. He reached out a trembling hand and brushed his fingers against my cheek. "Shit."

Whist finally released me, but they boxed me in, leaving me no way to escape. And a part of me didn't want to. A part of me craved their touch. With Whist no longer wrapped around me, the ache returned to my chest. A hollow emptiness, like a part of me was missing.

I huddled into myself, wrapping my arms around my middle. "W-what's going on? What do you mean you're supposed to kill me? Who are you?"

Whist threw more wood on my fire, making it blaze back to life. I could see the three of them better and it made my heart pound harder, faster. They were beautiful, like carved statues come to life. They could have broken me in half with ease.

I scooted back against the log, hugging my feet to my chest and waited for answers.

The three men sat in a half circle in front of me, close but not touching. Why did I want them to touch me?

The one with the voice pointed to Whist. "He's Whistler, but we call him Whist. That one is Schuyler, but we call him Sky. And I'm Saber."

"I'm Rhapsody." My voice came out trembling and small and confused.

"We know." Whist inspected me like some sort of fascinating specimen.

I sat up, frowning. "How do you know who I am?"

"We were sent by the king." Sky tossed another branch onto the fire.

I watched the sparks dance and flicker in the air instead of watching them. "Why?"

A long silence fell around us before Whist answered my question. "We're assassins."

My head whipped back around to face the men, shock stiffening my body. "He wants me dead? Why? I have done nothing illegal."

Saber sighed and rubbed the back of his neck. "Which is why he sent us."

My brow furrowed, and I shook my head, not understanding. "But... if he wants me dead, why am I still alive?"

"You don't know? You don't feel it?" Sky asked.

"Know what?"

Whist speared me with his gaze, his starlight eyes burning through me. "We're your kindreds."

A loud ringing blared through my mind, my thoughts tripping over themselves. This couldn't be happening. "No. That's impossible. No. Sorry, but I don't believe in kindreds."

Whist jerked back. "How can you not believe in kindreds?"

I pinched the bridge of my nose and tried to straighten my mind, my thoughts. "I mean, I believe they're real and all, but I don't believe in being forced to be with them. Don't you know why the king wants me dead? Have you not heard my songs?"

Whist snarled and ran his hand through his hair. "Oh, we've heard your songs. They've reached everywhere, people whisper them and pass them along. They have the palace in an uproar."

Saber slid a hand up my arm. "Don't you feel it? The heat between us? The rightness?"

I swallowed hard, trying to ignore the goosebumps rising in the wake of his hand, and shook off his touch. "It doesn't matter."

Saber smiled in understanding. "Oh, love it matters. Now that we've met you, touched you. It'll rip us to shreds if you try to deny the connection."

I shook my head. No. This could not happen. "I'll get over it and so will you."

Sky patted my knee. "We can keep you safe. When we don't return the king will send more after you."

I jerked away from him, trying desperately to ignore the heat his touch sent racing through my body. "I'll be more careful, but I will not stop performing."

Sky's hand clenched into a fist, like he was trying not to reach out for me again. "You have to. The king doesn't want your words causing an uprising."

I scoffed with bitterness. "I highly doubt he needs to worry about that."

"You'd be surprised." Saber clapped his hand onto Sky's shoulder and the tension bled out of him.

Interesting.

Whist kicked dirt onto the fire. "Enough. Try to go back to sleep. We'll talk more tomorrow and take you to a safe place until we figure out our next move."

Did they really expect me to sleep? Did they really expect me to just go along with them when I'd never seen them before in my life and had no idea the type of men they were? All I knew was they were assassins, and that was certainly not a ringing endorsement.

My chances of slipping away undetected were slim. One would remain awake, on guard while the rest of us slept. How could I convince them to let me go?

Ignoring them, I curled up under my blanket, hiding my face. This couldn't be happening. What were the chances of me having three kindreds who were also assassins for the king? I hadn't expected to even had kindreds since my parents weren't bonded. The other few bastards I'd met hadn't found theirs.

I faked sleep, listening to them chat quietly.

"What the fuck are we going to do? We didn't come prepared for this. And in a week, we'll have prices on our heads along with hers." Sky sounded worried and frustrated.

Saber sighed. "I don't know. I can't believe we share the same kindred. I never dared hope we could stay together." Saber's voice and words drew me to him, but I fought it off.

"We will take her to one of my safe houses and lie low for a few weeks. Maybe once she's disappeared, the king will forget about her." Whist sounded certain and determined, not a hint of doubt coloring his tone.

"Unlikely, if we don't return," Saber said.

Sky scoffed. "We aren't his slaves, we're his employees. We can quit whenever we want."

"Should we run? Head to Havisam?" Saber asked.

I smothered a snort. No way in hell was I running away to another country.

"It would still be a risk. Well-known royal assassins show up there? They could declare war." Whist said.

"We'll do whatever it takes to keep her safe. Most people have no idea what we look like. We have forged papers, supplies all over the country." Sky has lost all of his humor.

"She doesn't seem to want to go anywhere with us." Saber pointed out the obvious. He was the only one who seemed to give a shit about my opinions.

"She'll change her mind. She clearly doesn't have any idea what it's like to be kindred. Why did her parents not prepare her?" Sky certainly was confident. I looked forward to seeing his confidence shattered.

"Maybe she's an orphan." Again, Saber was the only one who was thinking of my feelings instead of how to control me.

Sky made a thoughtful humming sound. "Probably. She's angry enough at the royals to have some sort of trauma in her past."

"Don't we all." Whist was dismissive, focused on my safety and their next moves.

"Don't be a dick, Whist. Three men appeared in the night to kill her and then declared her their kindred. Her entire life is being upended. It's a lot for anyone to take in."

"We just lost our well-paying jobs, have to leave our home, and go on the run to keep our criminal kindred safe. She isn't the only one having to make do." A small pang of guilt slid through me at Whist's words.

"Yes, but we have actually been looking for our kindred. She has apparently been running from finding hers. We need to understand what happened to make her this way. Was there anything in her file that would explain it?" Sky seemed to find his empathy.

Whist cursed. "There's precious little on her. The only thing we know is her first name, description, and the lyrics to most of her songs. They had no info on family or friends. She has no home. She just travels from village to village passing along her borderline seditious prose."

"But look at her. She's perfect and gorgeous and deadly and brave. Everything we could ever want in a kindred." Saber's voice was filled with longing.

"Other than the criminal side of her." Sky snorted. "But you're right. She's everything we hoped for other than her complete disinterest in joining us."

Their conversation wound down as they each sank into their own thoughts. It sounded like they were settling in for the remainder of the night. It was time for me to think, to plan, to escape.

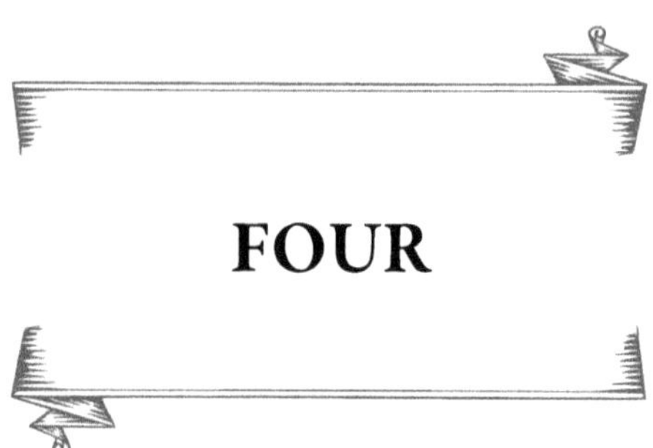

FOUR

I woke with a jolt, sitting up so fast my head spun. When did I fall asleep? I had planned to wait them out and try to sneak away. How was I even comfortable enough to sleep surrounded by three strange men?

"Good morning. Hungry?" Sky's blue eyes twinkled at me with humor. There was no sign of Saber or Whist.

"I'm fine." The morning air held a chill, and I eyed the fire with longing.

"Stubborn one, aren't you?" He quirked a smile at me.

"I ran out of supplies. I was planning on restocking today in the next village."

"We have plenty of supplies. Eat something. You're too thin." His eyes flicked over my body. Judging from the heat in his gaze, my thinness didn't bother him too much.

I glared at him. "I said I'm fine."

He held his hands up in surrender. "Whatever you say. But Whist makes really delicious campfire eggs. We even have a little bacon."

My mouth watered. I'd only had tinned food and stale bread and dried cheese recently. But no. I refused to accept anything from them. It would put me in their debt and that was a place I couldn't afford to be. I pulled my precious bottle of brandy from my pack and took a swig. The smoky liquid warmed me from the inside and made some of my tension bleed away.

"Can't say I disapprove of your type of breakfast." Sky stretched his arms high above his head, making his shirt ride up and giving me a glimpse of toned skin. I studied him in the morning light. He had a dark mop of curls on the top of his head and his eyes matched the color of the summer sky perfectly. His skin was sun-kissed and spread over rippling muscles. Lean, but not an ounce of extra padding on him. How did someone so gorgeous make a decent assassin? How did he hide in plain sight? From what I saw in the darkness the night before, the other two were just as attractive. Did the king like to surround himself with beauty?

I shoved the bottle back in my pack, not liking the way he eyed my brandy. Or me. I was certainly not sharing. It was the one luxury I allowed myself. "Where are the others?"

"They went to scout the area and make sure there aren't any guards around."

I folded my blanket and returned it to my pack. "You three should really return to the palace and just forget you ever knew me."

"Not going to happen, doll."

"You can't force the kindred on me." I whipped my cloak around my shoulders and tied my boots.

Sky smiled. "True, but we can follow you around and be generally annoying until you give in."

I narrowed my eyes at him. "That's called stalking."

He shrugged with careless grace. "I prefer to look at it as wooing."

"I'm headed to the next village. You'll have to kidnap me to stop me." I raised my chin, daring him to try.

"We aren't going to kidnap you. Well, Whist might consider it, but I won't let him. But you really should reconsider. It's dangerous."

"Is it? The king sent you three for me. How is he supposed to know you already found me?"

"We weren't the only ones sent to find you, doll. If the royal guard finds you first, they're to bring you to the palace."

None of it made sense. I wasn't a revolutionary leader, I was just a traveling bard who played controversial music. "What I'm doing isn't illegal."

"No, which is why he sent us. To make you disappear. The royal guards will bring you in for questioning and then there will be some tragic accident in the dungeons."

"And you three always do his dirty work for him? Take out innocent citizens for daring to disagree with the royals?"

"Usually, our jobs are a bit more... specific to national security. We take out spies and assassins from other countries, threats to the royals. This was a first for us." A hint of deadly seriousness peeked from behind his mask of humor. It didn't look like their mission sat well with him. Which was something I could work to my advantage.

"You were still going to go through with it before you realized I'm your kindred. Why would I want to join myself with people like that? Who obey without question even if it's unlawful or immoral?"

His mask of humor returned as he shot me a silly grin. "Because we're dashing and mysterious and no one will make you as happy as we will."

"That's not enough for me."

He moved close, so close the heat from his body seeped into mine, his lips a breath away. "Because no one will make you feel like we can. The pleasure we can wring from your body will have you begging us for more. Anyone from your past will pale in comparison from just a simple touch from one of us."

I swallowed hard as shivers raced up and down my spine. My nipples tightened at the dark promise in his eyes, in his voice. I leaned towards him a little, unable to fight the draw.

He wasn't grinning like a fool anymore, his expression filled with want. His hands reached for my waist and drew me even closer until I was plastered against him. We fit together like he was one of my missing pieces. His scent surrounded me—sunshine and blueberries. My body sang out with triumph and bliss at being in his arms.

He pressed a kiss at the junction of my neck and shoulder. I bit back a whimper as heat pooled low in my belly. His lips trailed up my neck and along my jaw, working me into a trembling state. I should've pulled away. I didn't want to give in to this connection. But my body had more than given in, it reached for it.

"Kiss me." His voice was a rough command, hardening my nipples farther, making me gasp.

Unable to disobey, I brought my lips to his, and he devoured me, consuming each moan, whimper, gasp. He nipped at my bottom lip, his tongue warring me mine, conquering me.

Against my kindreds, I lost my free will. Which was one of my major problems with kindreds.

His hands slid up my waist and his thumbs grazed the underside of my breasts. I arched against him, craving his touch higher, rougher.

A growl rumbled in his chest and his hands cupped my aching mounds, plucking at my nipples through the fabric of my clothes. I rubbed my legs together, desperate to relieve the ache at my center.

It had been such a long time since anyone had touched me like this.

My brain restarted, and I jerked away from him, almost falling on my ass, breathing hard. I brushed my fingers against my swollen lips. I was no prude, I had nothing against a little fun with a pretty fellow I'd never see again, but this was different. I wouldn't be able to simply rid myself of these assassins. If I gave in, the connection would be complete and they'd never let me go. And I wouldn't be able to hide from them for long.

Sky stared at me with dark eyes, the light blue color darkened with his lust. I grasped at the rock my hand brushed against and without thinking it through, I swung my arm as hard as I could, the stone connecting with Sky's temple with a sickening crunch.

FIVE

The resulting pain almost sent me into unconsciousness alongside of him, but I fought it off. Kindreds experienced any physical pain they caused the other. Too bad it didn't prevent emotional pain in the same way. Dizziness clouded my head for a moment and I clenched my teeth at the brandy burning my stomach, trying to claw back up my throat.

I hoped I didn't hurt Sky too badly. I just needed a head start.

Scrambling to my feet, I shoved the rest of my belongings into my pack and set off in the opposite direction of the town I planned to visit. There was another not too much farther from here. Hopefully, they'd search for me in the other village and I'd be long gone by the time they figured out where I was. One more job, stock up on supplies, then I'd take their advice and lie low for a bit.

They needed to understand I had no interest in being their kindred, no matter what my body wanted. They'd have to get over it.

The farther I got from them, the deeper the emptiness, the tighter the tension grew. My head still pounded from my assault on Sky. I shouldn't have kissed hum. It made the connection stronger. I did my best to ignore it, shoving the pain to the back of my mind, singing my songs under my breath to remind myself of the life I chose and the life I definitely did not want.

The last thing I wanted was to tie myself to assassins who did the king's dirty work, regardless of them disobeying for me. It had nothing to do with me and everything to do with the bond. Kindreds couldn't physically hurt each other without experiencing great pain themselves. If I'd killed him, I'd be dead too.

Worry gnawed at my belly. Worry I hurt him badly. Worry they'd find me. Worry the royal guards would be waiting for me. Worry I made the wrong choice.

I couldn't banish the reminder of how it felt to be pressed up against Sky, how his hands roved on me, how he tasted, smelled. What were Whist and Saber like?

Too bad I'd never know.

My breaths came a little easier once the village was in sight. I slipped my hood over my head to keep my face hidden and strode towards the market stalls. It only took me a few minutes to barter for enough supplies to last me at least a week if I was careful. Unfortunately, I had to forgo another bottle of brandy in favor of more nutritious items. With my pack full, I retreated towards the woodline, munching on a fresh roll. I hoped I could work in the tavern for the midday crowd. The faster I got in and out of there, the better. But I needed the job for more than my politics with the rest of my money spent on food.

I hid my pack beneath some brush and returned to the town, eyes open for the assassins or the guards. The only thing in the village were people going about their lives. On the surface, this was a prosperous and happy village, filled with kindred souls and their families.

But in every village there was a dark underbelly, something no one acknowledges in anything but whispers. There was the kindredless, the abused, the widowed. Most of whom weren't welcome into society. They were the ignored and forgotten, the dregs. They were who I played for even if they weren't there to hear.

I pushed open the tavern door and took a seat at the bar. "Brandy, please." I parted with my last coin. Might as well buy something I enjoyed.

The bartender poured a glass and pushed it across the counter. "Here ya go."

"Thanks."

She eyed the instrument on my back. "You're a musician?"

I took a sip of my drink before replying. "I am. I'd be willing to play for your midday meal crowd in exchange for a coin or two or a hot meal."

She pursed her lips in thought. "You any good?"

"I have had no complaints about my skill." My lyrics, yes. But never my skill.

She drummed her fingers against the counter. "I'll give you a hot meal and you can keep your coin for the drink and I'll add a second with your lunch."

Not as much as I hoped, but it'd have to do. At least I had enough food to last me a bit and the coin back in case of emergency. And it'd been a long time since I'd had hot and fresh food.

I nod. "Deal."

"Go take a seat in the corner and I'll bring your food to you."

I waited in a seat by the window with my back to the wall so I could see the villagers passing by and everyone inside the tavern. Those assassins were crafty. I wouldn't put it past them to figure out where I was. I needed to get out of there as soon as I could. I considered starting with some less offensive songs first so I didn't make a stir and draw attention.

No.

I refused to change my set or let the king make me afraid. He wouldn't shut me up. Not until he sent assassins who would actually finish the job. Until then, I would keep going. For my parents, for the dregs of society.

The bartender brought over a steaming bowl of bordello stew with a large hunk of fresh bread and a slice of blueberry pie. A pang stabbed my chest as the scent of blueberry wafted to my nose, reminding me of Sky.

I nodded in thanks and tucked in to the delicious food. I finished every bite, using the bread to soak up the last bit of stew, but the emptiness remained even as my hunger eased.

I carried the dirty dishes over to the bar and handed them over. "I'll get started now, if you want."

"Please. Hopefully, you'll pull some extra customers in here."

Feeling guilty, I began my set with my version of a popular song, one everyone in Faligrey knew. I played it differently, but it was still recognizable. My music trickled through the open windows and customers trickled through the door, putting in their orders, mouthing along to the song.

The bartender grinned over at me and I threw her another bone. Her food was superb. Besides, the more people I tempted with regular bar songs, the more people would hear my message.

A few coins landed in my hat and I was even more at ease. Changing my plans and coming to this village instead worked out perfectly.

I moved into one of my originals and no one acted offended, they still seemed to enjoy the show. It energized me and my voice rose.

A hush fell and then the muttering began. Just like usual. I knew it was too good to be true. Even after softening them up, they still didn't want to hear what the world was really like. They were blind to the truth. They were comfortable living the lie because the law worked for them, it didn't affect them negatively like it did so many of us. They didn't want free will and choices. It was easier this way.

I noticed the bartender from the corner of my eye staring at me with a smile on her face. At least I didn't seem to be offending her. I guessed she'd gotten her pay from the crowd, it didn't matter if they left in offense now.

My confidence plummeted when four royal guardsmen stomped through the door.

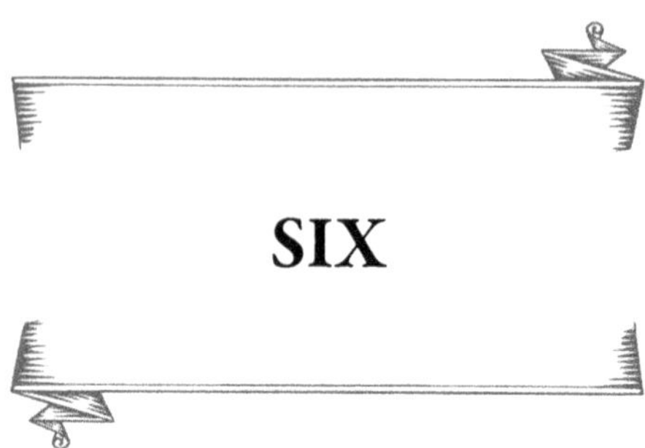

SIX

My strings almost snapped beneath my fingers. I grasped my ukulele and raced for the back exit. The bartender moved out of my way, instead of blocking me like I expected.

One of the guards seized the back of my cloak, but I kicked back at him, smashing him right in the knee with the heel of my boot. He screamed in pain and I ripped away from him, barreling through the back door and sprinting for the woods where I hid my pack.

Someone grabbed me around the waist and yanked me into a body carrying a familiar scent. Sunshine and blueberries.

Sky.

I relaxed against him, the assassins less of a threat than the royal guards, the constant ache disappearing at his touch. The void filled back up. Damn this connection. Damn it straight to hell.

"You plan to knock me out again, doll?" He whispered the question into my ear.

"Not at the moment. I have bigger problems." I fought against my body's desire to press back into him.

"Nothing you need to concern yourself with. Saber and Whist are handling it."

He set me down and spun me around. I winced at the dried blood and swelling on the side of his face.

"Sorry." I did mean it. And not just because of how much it hurt me.

"You can make it up to me later." His eyes smoldered at me and I tried to hide my shivery reaction. It was ridiculous how my body responded to him, to all three of them.

With more of an effort than I would ever admit to, I pulled away from him. "I need to get my pack."

"Where is it?"

I gestured behind me. "I hid it in the woods."

"Lead on, doll."

After taking stock of our surroundings, I headed toward my hiding spot. I still didn't want to hide away with three assassins, but I was also not interested in being arrested and taken to the palace. Maybe lying low with them for a while was a good idea. They were clearly not going to leave me alone. And I couldn't run from them and the royal guard.

"You can't run from us again. We can't keep you safe if you keep performing like this." Sky's words echoed my thoughts.

Which did nothing but bring out my contrariness. "I don't need you to keep me safe."

He rolled his eyes as he held back a low-hanging branch for me. "Sure. You're doing great on your own. But now that Saber and Whist have dealt with the guards, word will get back to the king faster than we wanted. We're blown, and that makes things even hotter for you. We're your best chance at getting through this alive."

I blew out a sigh as I dug out my pack. He had a point. If I hid out for a bit, maybe things would calm down and the king would forget about me. I was just some bard, not a threat to the country. It wasn't like I was the leader of some uprising.

But if I stayed with the assassins, I could lose myself in them. I didn't know how long I'd be able to hold out against the feelings they brought out in me. I didn't know what to do.

"Fine. I'll stay with you three. For now."

Sky took my arm. "Come on. We need to put some distance between us and this town."

I stumbled in his wake. "What about the others?"

He steadied me and slowed his pace. "We have a rendezvous spot planned. They'll meet us there."

"What if more guards come?"

Sky laughed, loud and long and hard.

"What's so amusing?" My voice was sharp with annoyance. Did he take anything seriously?

"The thought of those two not being able to handle a few guards. Hell, a few dozen guards won't be a problem. We're assassins, doll."

I hopped over a small fallen tree. "Exactly. You're not soldiers. You sneak around in shadows and alleys and kill people before they even know you're there."

He chuckled. "You've been reading too many novels. Granted, we do handle it that way sometimes, we're also trained in battle. Don't worry, they'll be just fine."

The sun dipped toward the horizon, the days already growing shorter. Dark would be on us in less than two hours

"Maybe I should hope for the opposite. That way there's only you to deal with and then I'm two steps closer to being free." The words tasted wrong in my mouth, but I said them anyway. Maybe if I resisted loudly and often, I would convince myself.

He yanked me closer until all I could smell was him. "You don't mean that, doll. It's a lot to wrap your mind around. Believe me I understand."

"I don't think you do." I tried to catch my bearings, but Sky had lead and turned me in so many different directions, I was completely turned around.

"Why don't you explain it to me then? Why are you so against kindred souls?"

"I'm not really against them. I believe they're real. And I even believe they work out happily for some people. But I don't believe we should be forced together. And I don't believe you should only be allowed to marry and have a family with kindreds. We should have choices and opportunities to decide for ourselves. So many people don't even find their kindreds and they're forced to spend their lives alone, never having children. It's bullshit."

"But what about people who find their kindreds later in life? What if they're married and have a family? What happens then?"

I shrugged. "Multiple mates are common. They can make it work."

"But a kindred connection is much more powerful than a relationship without it. It would overshadow it." There was something I couldn't read or understand in his expression. Something hopeful? Excited? Relieved? I wasn't sure. But I was beginning to think my views made him happy.

"Perhaps. Perhaps they could make it work. But it would be their choice. They could choose to wait and search for their kindred or they could choose to accept love when they find it."

"Maybe you're right. But doll, I have to tell you. If you were already in a relationship with someone, I'd want to kill him. Not share you with him. I'm already going to have to share you with my best mates."

I scowled, tired of repeating myself. "I haven't decided to give in to the connection. You can't force me."

All signs of humor disappear from his face. "We'd never force you. Ever."

"Good. I'd kill anyone who tried."

A huge smile lit up his face, his eyes sparkling with delight. "Oh, doll. I completely understand how we're kindred."

"What do you mean?" I asked.

"He means you're just as blood-thirsty as us and he likes it."

I jumped, whirling around at the voice behind me.

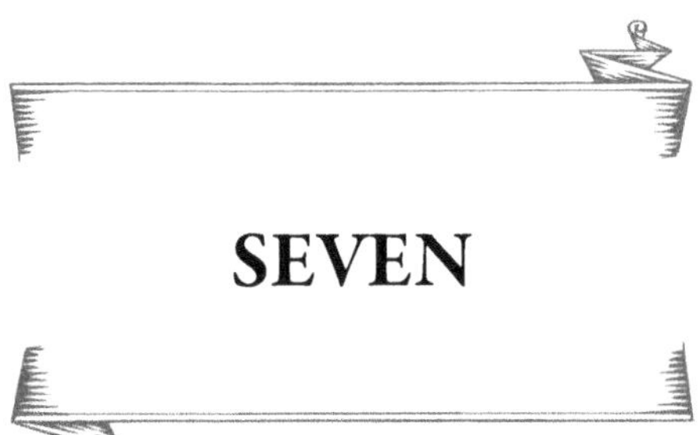

SEVEN

Whistler.

He scowled at me. "Are you finished being a stubborn, hard-headed ass?"

I tossed my head. "For now. No promises on tomorrow."

Whist tried to hide it, but I still saw the smile haunting his eyes. His really beautiful eyes. They burned through me like starlight every time he looked at me. Everything about him was beautiful. His dark red hair, pale skin with a scattering of freckles in delightful and surprising places, the lean muscles bulging against his shirt, the hard, stubborn jaw and sharp cheekbones, his plush and kissable lips.

Kissable lips? What was I thinking? Why were my thoughts constantly running away from me? I did not want to be overtaken by lust and the kindred bond until I was mindless with wanting them. I hadn't even known them a full day yet. It was way too soon for any kind of commitments.

Saber pressed into my side, his arm brushing against me. "We need to get moving. It will take us a few hours to get to the safe house."

"We're going on foot? And we aren't going farther than a few hours from here?" We should have been getting as far away as fast as possible.

Whist retied his boot. "Yes, on foot. We can't travel on main roads. And it's well-hidden and we need to be out of sight now. Better to lay low than to remain out in the open."

I shrugged. "I'm used to traveling on foot."

"Good. Let's go." Whist and the others suddenly had packs on their backs. When did that happen? Where did they come from?

Whist took the lead and Sky took the rear, leaving Saber walking next to me. He remained close, his body almost in constant contact with mine. It both calmed me and wound me up somehow. I couldn't get as good a read on him as the other two assassins. Sky was all cockiness and humor with the occasional flash of deadly dominance. Whist was pure angry alpha, the determined leader. But Saber, I didn't know. He'd shown flashes of humor, but he said little, choosing instead to observe and follow the other's leads. What did he see when he watched everything so closely? What did he see in me?

That was another problem I had with kindreds. Supposedly, the magic joining us together meant our personalities were perfect matches. But how was I supposed to be a perfect match for three such different men? I wanted to be loved for who I was, not because some mystical forced us together. Like my parents. They chose each other. Over and over again, they chose each other. They might not have been perfect matches in the eyes of our world, but they were to each other.

Was I supposed to ignore everything I learned from them, everything this cruel world taught me and give in like the masses? Just because I found three gorgeous men who made my heart pound and palms sweat and every inch of me crave their touch?

My parents could never describe how overpowering it was since they never experienced it. And it's not like I had extended family or friends to explain it. My parents were banished and disowned as soon as they got married.

Lost in my morbid thoughts, I stumbled over a root and Saber reached out to steady me, then tucked my arm into his.

"I can walk on my own."

"I know. But I like touching you. It eases me."

I refused to admit it eased me too. I breathed him in, almost closing my eyes in rapture. He smelled smoky and smooth, like campfire and my favorite brandy. I wanted to lick him all over. His brown skin was a few shades darker than my bronze tone, his black hair cropped close to his head, a nasty scar cut into the middle of his cheek from his eye to his upper lip made him seem dangerous and mysterious, his body tall and broad with a tapered waist leading to tight trousers showing off his other assets.

I pressed closer into him and he looked over at me with a soft smile, his dark brown eyes overflowing with secrets. Secrets I wanted to uncover.

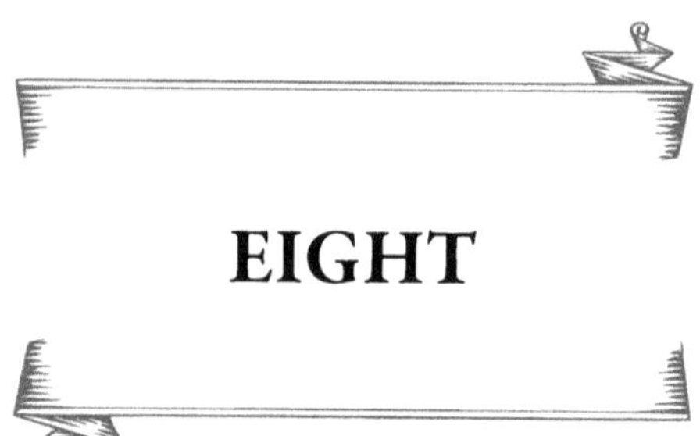

EIGHT

My legs and back ached, and I wanted nothing more than to curl up on the ground and go to sleep. Everything from the last couple days had caught up to me, leaving me empty and exhausted, torn and confused. After I got some sleep, maybe I'd be able to think clearly and decide what to do next.

Because right at the moment, I had no idea.

I bit back a groan as we climbed up a hill. I would not admit how tired I was. Saber pulled away from me and took my hand, threading our fingers together. My stomach swooped, but I kept my expression bland and my eyes glued ahead.

At the top of the hill, I could see down into a small valley filled with trees of every color. The waning light of the sun set the valley on fire. A small cottage sat in the middle of the trees, small and quaint. Was this the safe house? Not at all what I expected. It was charming, like something out of the books I read as a child.

With the end of our journey in sight, a burst of energy crashed through me and my steps hastened on our way down the hill. I hoped they had a bath in there. I couldn't remember the last time I bathed in anything other than cold streams and rivers.

Saber led me up onto the small covered porch while Whist unearthed the key from a hiding place behind one of the shutters and unlocked the door.

It was musty and dusty inside, but otherwise neat and clean and welcoming. Sunlight filtered through the windows, lighting up the dust motes. The cottage was small, one main room with a sofa and two plush chairs and a small eating and cooking area towards the back. Three closed doors led to other rooms and hopefully a washroom.

"Make yourself at home, doll. The middle door is the washroom if you want a bath. The door on the left will be your room if you want." Sky gestured to the closed door.

"Where will the rest of you sleep?" Not with me.

Sky grinned. "Saber and I will share the other bedroom and Whist usually takes the sofa anyway."

Whist probably wanted to guard the door. From invasion and to keep me from escaping. I'd bide my time. I was no moron. They were my safest option for the time being. They'd do anything to keep me safe. There would come a point where they let their guard down and I'd have the chance to disappear.

I closed myself inside the room Sky pointed out, breathing deeply at finally being alone. Since they were just in the next room and I wasn't trying to get away from them, my body didn't protest the separation. There was a slight emptiness, but nothing as uncomfortable as before. If I gave into the bond, the pain and uncomfortable sensations would lessen and eventually fade. It was the bond trying to force the connection.

And I did not like being forced.

Instead of rejoining the assassins after my bath, I pulled out some of my food and munch it on my new bed. The room was basic—a surprisingly large bed in the center of the wood floors, a small set of drawers in the corner, a green rug by the bed, a small table with a lantern and a few candles. I locked the door leading into the washroom since both bedrooms had private access to the washroom and I didn't want any surprise guests.

Once I finished my meager dinner, I brushed away the crumbs and slid under the covers. I didn't know how the assassins set up this house or why, but it wasn't a bad place to hide out. I sank into the plush mattress, choosing a spot right in the middle of the massive bed.

All three assassins could have easily fit in there with me and left room to spare.

I shoved away the thought and just enjoyed being in a real bed. I was so used to the hard forest floor as a bed, I wasn't sure I'd be able to sleep on something so soft. But it was so glorious and comfortable, I was unwilling to move.

It didn't take long for sleep to find me.

I floated away on my bed of clouds, feeling safe for the first time, maybe ever.

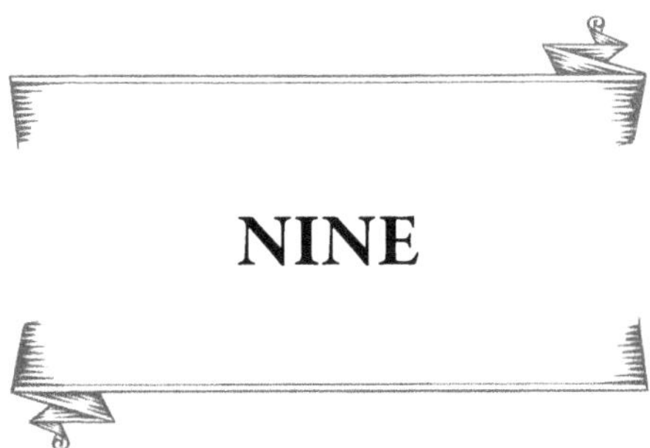

NINE

I woke to a soft stroke on my cheek and a quiet voice. "Rhapsody, love. There's food if you're hungry."

With a reluctant groan, I rolled over and squinted open my eyes. "How did you get in here? I locked the doors."

Saber smiled at me. "I'm an assassin. Locked door won't stop me."

I frowned in disapproval. "Just because you can, doesn't mean you should."

His continued strokes on my face, on my arms soothed me. "I did knock, but you didn't answer. You've been shut in here for fifteen hours. We were getting a little worried you ran out on us again."

"Like Whist doesn't have some kind of alarm system set up outside my window for just that scenario." I snorted and sat up.

"Maybe."

I scoffed and shoved back the covers to climb from the bed. "I won't be a prisoner."

"You aren't one. If, in a few days, you are determined to ignore the bond of kindred souls and go on with your life without us, we will have to adjust. We will never force you to remain with us and lock you away to keep you safe. I can't promise we'll be able to stay away from you, but we'll watch from afar if that's what you really want. All we ask is you give us a chance. Get to know us. Let us keep you safe until this mess with the king calms down. You don't have to hide in here the whole time. We don't bite." He grinned, his eyes twinkling. "Unless you want us to."

My breath caught at the vision his words brought to my mind. I shook it off and grabbed my cloak to ward against the chill in the air. Autumn was quickly moving into winter, the worst time of year for me. It was miserable sleeping in the elements.

Something to consider with my new kindreds determined to take care of me. Not that I needed to be taken care of. Since before my parents died, I learned to rely on only myself.

I couldn't forget that just because I had three dangerous men who tempted me more than was good for me.

Saber trailed me into the main room where I found Sky sprawled on the sofa and Whist standing over the wood-burning stove making something that smelled utterly heavenly. He glanced over his shoulder, still stirring whatever he was making, and looked me up and down, something I didn't recognize swirling in the depths of his starlight eyes.

My stomach rumbled, making Whist snort. "It'll be ready in about three minutes. There's bread on the table if you need something now."

I eyed the bread, but shook my head. "I can wait. I had some food before I slept. What are you making?"

"Steak and eggs. Fried apples and cream for dessert."

My mouth watered and my eyes actually almost teared up. I didn't realize how much I missed real, fresh food.

Sky leapt from the sofa and approached the table, sliding out a chair for me. "Have a seat, doll."

My brows furrowed in irritation, but I sat. "Thanks."

Sky and Saber took the seats on either side of mine, crowding me with their massive bodies. My pulse fluttered at their scents of sunshine and blueberries, campfire and brandy.

What did Whist smell like? I couldn't remember from the other night when he was wrapped around me and he'd kept his distance since. I studied him as he finished up breakfast or whatever meal this is. He was precise and his expression calm, like cooking was his bliss. He chopped fresh herbs and added them to the pan, the meat sizzling and spitting.

Sky noticed my interest. "Our boy over there loves cooking. His mother is a palace chef and he's almost as good as her. I've been telling him for years he should retire and open up a tavern."

Whist spoke without turning around. "That would ruin it."

Sky scowled playfully at Whist's back. "I told you we'd retire with you and run the business end of things."

"And what do either of you know about running a business?" Whist asked in a dry voice.

"Nothing. But we're fast learners. And look, we've stumbled across the entertainment." Sky gestured at me with a grin. "Besides, we may not have a choice now." Sky winked at me to soften his words, but guilt slid through me anyway.

I'd been so focused on the changes everything was bringing to my life, I kept ignoring what it had done to their lives. They had good lives working for the king, killing people who need killing, apparently enough money to set up luxurious safe houses. Now, they were outlaws just like me, on the run, no home.

At least they had each other. That was more than I'd had since my parents died.

"There are always other choices. We'll figure it out. The king will understand we couldn't finish the job."

My head jerked up. "He'll just have someone else kill me."

Whist plopped a platter of steaming food onto the table. "Which is why we have no plans to bring you to him. If we end up having to return, we'll hide you somewhere."

I breathed in the scents of the food, hunger pangs shooting through my stomach. "I'm not spending the rest of my life hidden away like a shameful secret."

Saber placed his warm hand over mine. "We're not going to ask you to. Not long-term. Just for now. We've bought ourselves some time to figure everything out."

I slid my hand away from Saber, hating the shivers and butterflies his touch causes me. "How did the three of you end up becoming assassins anyway?"

"It's a long and rather depressing story." Sky exchanged a glance with Saber.

"Apparently we're stuck together for a while. We have the time. And depressing stories don't scare me."

"We're more worried you'll turn our story into another political protest song." Whist filled a plate and placed it in front of me.

I stared at the food, forcing myself to wait until everyone else was served. "All art is political. Whether on purpose or not, your beliefs and morals sink into your work."

"Yours just seems to have a little extra than the average artist."

"Stop trying to change the subject." I pursed my lips into a frown aimed at Sky.

Sky stared at my lips, his eyes darkening to sapphires. "We'll tell you ours if you tell us yours."

I cleared my throat and fidgeted in my seat. "Deal. But you first."

We tucked into the food Whist made and I smothered the groan rising in my chest. It was delicious. The steak was buttery and so soft I didn't even need the knife beside my plate. The eggs were fluffy and fragrant with herbs. And the apples, oh my word, the apples. They were still a bit crisp and tart with honey and spices sweetening them, the cold cream melting against the heat.

I barely inhaled as I shoveled it into my mouth, forgetting the manners my father tried to instill in me. The assassins watched me with varying shades of amusement and awe and concern.

I took a moment to swallow my mouthful. "What?"

"How long has it been since you've had a proper meal?" Saber asked.

Heat stung my cheeks. "I eat plenty. Just never this delicious."

Sky waved a piece of steak in the air. "All the more reason to stay with us. You can eat like this all the time."

I eyed their trim and muscular figures. "How is it the three of you are in such good shape if you eat like this all the time?"

"We train a lot." Whist deadpanned.

I rolled my eyes. "Of course." I sipped at the wine Whist served with the meal. "So, assassins. How does one get a job in that field?"

The three of them glanced at each other before somehow Whist was somehow elected to tell the story. "We were soldiers. We were excellent soldiers. We ended up in the elite squad in the king's inner circle. After a few assassination attempts on his life, the king realized he needed his own assassins to deal with threats quietly. So, the three of us along with a handful of others were chosen to train in the art of killing."

That was it? The whole story? It told me nothing. "How is that a long and depressing tale? It was more boring than anything."

"Yeah, Whist. You left out all the drama. How we were almost executed. How the assassins almost killed us and the prince and princess. How we had no choice but to become assassins or we would have faced execution." There was a dark edge to Sky's humor. One that made me think Saber wasn't the only one with secrets hidden behind his eyes.

I had always loved uncovering secrets.

"If that's true, why are you so loyal to the king? Why haven't you left and started over in another country?"

"We still have people, family we care about. We can't move them all. And we aren't the only assassins who work for the king. They'll track us down. Besides, we're loyal to the princess. She's a much better person than her father and will be a far superior ruler. He's old. He'll die soon enough." Whist shrugged.

"You're waiting for the day the princess gives you the order to kill him?" Would the princess actually change anything?

Whist heaved a rather depressed sigh. "She won't. Unfortunately."

"What about you, doll? Why are you so against kindreds?" Sky asked.

I nibbled on my bottom lip and push my plate away, hunger vanishing. "My parents weren't kindreds."

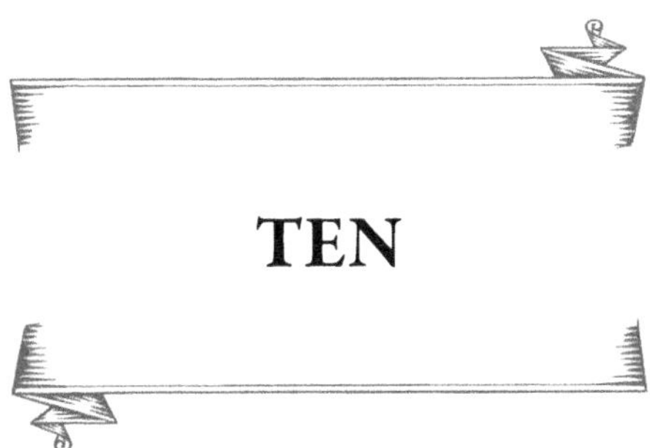

TEN

I didn't know what I felt after I gave them a brief retelling of my personal history. I couldn't tell what they felt either. There was a hollow sensation in my chest, but an oddly comforting one. Like the weight I carried everywhere had lifted.

Was I so lonely? So lonely that as soon as I unburdened myself, as soon as I trusted someone with the bare minimal information of my past, as soon as I let someone the slightest bit inside, I took whatever scraps they offered?

Why did I trust them so easily? It couldn't be the bond causing it all. Nothing I'd heard and read about the kindred souls bond explained the trust. It explained the lust; it explained the attraction; it explained the comfort their presence brought me.

It didn't explain the trust. Especially for someone like me. They certainly didn't seem to trust me. At least, they didn't seem to trust me not to run, or put myself in danger. Which, fair enough.

And I didn't trust them to let me choose my own path. So I couldn't allow myself to grow too comfortable with them. I couldn't allow what seemed like three amazing men into my heart. I couldn't allow myself to give into the bond.

The men disappeared, leaving me alone with my thoughts. I needed to plan my next move. As lovely as it was there, it wasn't a long-term solution. For any of us.

I needed to convince them to forget about me, to let me go, to return to their lives.

Whist seemed the least interested happy about finding his kindred. He'd mostly stayed away from me since they found me. And he acted as the leader of their little merry band of assassins. If he agreed to let me live my life, the others would probably fall in line.

I slipped out the back door in the kitchen and past the clearing Sky was training in with his sword. Shirtless. Temptation pulled me in his direction, but I shook it off. It didn't matter how beautiful he was or how the sunlight glinted against the sheen of sweat on his chest. It didn't matter the laughter and lightness he'd already brought to my soul in such a short time.

I had to convince Whist the best thing for all of us was for us to go about our lives like we'd never met.

Darting away before Sky caught sight of me, I ducked behind the flowering bushes intertwined with vines of ivy that created a wall on a small white fence. It led to a path which led to a small vegetable garden.

And there was Whist, on his knees in the dirt.

Whist raised his head to watch me approach.

"You garden too?" I stopped a few feet from him.

He sat back on his heels, a soil-covered carrot hanging from his hand. "Of course. I'm pleased to see we still have crop left this late."

"Does that mean fresh vegetables for dinner?" I shifted from foot to foot, unsure how to broach the subject naturally and I'd never been great at small talk.

Instead of the usual starlight, his eyes brimmed with dark clouds. "It does. For several of them. I'll need to tin whatever we don't eat, so I have plenty to keep me busy while we hide out over the next few days."

"Wish I could say the same." I didn't take time off. I was always playing or traveling.

"Want to help?" He held out a spade.

I shrugged and accepted it, kneeling beside him. "I have no idea what I'm doing."

"You didn't have a garden growing up?" He dropped the carrot into a basket already overflowing with vegetables.

"We never lived in one place long enough to plant one. Did your mother teach you this too?" I breathed in the scents of sun-warmed soil, late-blooming flowers, and pine with closed eyes. I'd always loved the song of nature. It called to me, soothed me. Good thing, since I made my home outside.

"She did." His words brought me back to earth, pulling me away from the music only I can hear.

Something in his tone grabbed at me. "What about your father?"

Whist dug at the dirt, his fingers gentle. "He died when I was young. And my mother only had one kindred."

Most people only had one. Multiple matings wasn't unheard of or uncommon, but the majority still only had one kindred.

"So she's spent all this time alone?" Sadness welled in my chest. The poor woman. For decades, she'd been alone, unable to find another love because our king was a dick.

"She has." He stopped digging and stared at his filthy hands.

"And you don't see anything wrong with that?" I wanted to crack him open and read the thoughts in his brain. He kept his expression so closed down, shuttered.

His head whipped around so he could meet my eyes. "I never said that. I never said I disagreed with anything you said."

"So, you think the kindred souls are a racket too?" I turned my attention back to the vegetables, unable to bear the savage expression on his face.

Whist helped me unearth a potato. "Not at all. I just agree there should be choices instead of laws. Like there used to be and like there is in Havisam."

"What's waiting for you back at the palace?" I grinned at the potato in my hands. Gardening was rather fun.

"A life of killing for the king." There was no expression in his voice, no emotion. I couldn't figure out how he felt about his job, his life.

"Nothing else? Isn't your mother there?" He'd said she was the palace chef. Wouldn't he want to return to her? Especially since she apparently had no one else.

"Yes."

"Don't you want to go back to her? And go back and wait for the princess to take over and hopefully make things better?" If she ended up actually making things better instead of leaving it as it was. I knew little about her, but had yet to be impressed by the spoiled royals.

A small smile ghosted across his lips. "I'm not an idiot, gorgeous. You're not going to talk me into walking away from you and taking the other two with me."

My shoulders slumped, and I grumbled at being so easily read. Damn it. I had to argue him around to seeing things my way. "If you choose to stay with me, you're giving up your life. You may never see your mother again. And you'll end up dead because I'm not running. I won't quit fighting." I couldn't.

"My mother will be fine. The king won't punish her, she's special to the princess and prince. And we won't ask you to quit. But we'll do our best to keep you safe. We'll help you get in and out of villages. Help keep you hidden. We have these sorts of places all over the country."

It all sounded too good to be true, and I didn't trust a word. No way would it work. Eventually, they'd grow tired and resent me. "What kind of life is that for you?"

Whist let out a humorless snort. "One much better than the one we left."

"How can you mean that? Do you have any idea what life is like on the run?" It was hard, brutal, lonely.

"On the run? No. Always moving, always in danger, never staying in one place long, yes. We won't miss the palace because we're usually only there long enough to receive our next mission and set off again. And we usually aren't sent together, so now the three of us won't be separated any longer." Whist stabbed the spade into the ground with frustrated force.

I frowned. "But you just said last the other night about how your life has been turned upside down. I thought you'd want to return to it." He was supposed to be the one who wanted his life back.

Whist tangled his fingers with mine in the dirt as we dug up an onion. "The last thing I expected was to have one of our assignments turn out to be my kindred. And not just mine, but my two closest friends. It does change everything. But now that I've had time to get over the initial shock and wrap my head around it, I'm no longer frustrated."

My hands stilled beneath his, my heart pounding in my ears. "You're telling me you prefer it this way instead of your kindred being some bartender or tavern owner you could take back to the palace with you?"

"And what kind of life would we give her? One she spends alone in a beautiful house while we're constantly gone on missions? Or one where she's widowed young and has to spend the rest of her life alone like my mother? Or one where she travels with us and we get her killed? Trust me. If you were a bartender, we'd probably still be holed up here trying to figure out our next move." He eased the onion from the earth and tossed it into the basket, one of his hands still squeezing mine.

I stared at him, unsure what to think. Could it be so simple? If I agreed, could I have it all? A powerful relationship with these three men? Continue playing my music and honoring the memory of my parents?

Whistler rose to his feet gracefully, and after squeezing my shoulder, left me alone kneeling in the dirt to ponder over his words.

The man was smarter than I'd given him credit for.

ELEVEN

I tilted my head back so the sun could shine on my face, my hood falling around my shoulders. My mind whirled in dizzying circles as I tried to come to a decision.

I didn't know them well enough to believe Whistler's words. As much as I longed to, I couldn't quite do it. My entire life had trained me otherwise. I trusted them to a point, and maybe he meant them, but he wouldn't necessarily always feel the same way. He could change his mind. And then where would I be?

I stood and dusted myself off. The best plan was to wait and see how the business with the guards and other assassins shook out. No matter how much a large part of me wished to remain with them, another part of me rebelled against it. And that part was loud and frightened.

Sky stopped me before I could return inside. "Hey, doll. You all right?"

"Yeah. Fine." I scrubbed at the dirt on my hands instead of looking at his still bare and gleaming chest.

He tapped my chin with his pointer finger. "In all my experience, when someone says they're fine, they're always the exact opposite."

I shrugged. "Just trying to make some decisions." I raised my head to see his face.

He was clearly tempted to question me further, but he swallowed it. "Want to learn a few fight moves?"

My brows shot high on my forehead. "Why?"

"Because if you leave us, you need a way to protect yourself." He broke our gaze and swallowed hard.

I bit the inside of my cheek. It seemed like somehow I'd hurt him. "I've done all right so far."

His eyes twinkled with returned good humor. "Yes, but you have royal guards and assassins after you."

He had a point. "All right."

"Have you had any training?"

"I'm fairly decent with a knife." I fingered the dagger hidden up my sleeves.

"Show me." He gestured to the small backyard to the left of Whist's garden. "I have a target set up on the tree over there."

It was nothing but a simple board with a target painted in the middle nailed on the tree. I slid my dagger from my sleeve and sent it whirling at the board.

It sank right in the middle.

Sky whistled. "You weren't exaggerating even a little, were you, doll?"

"You doubted me?" I raised a brow at him with a smirk to match his own.

"A little." He laughed. "Something I should know better by now."

"Clearly." Something about Sky's company slipped past my boundaries and I let my guard down.

"Who taught you?"

"No one. I spend a lot of time alone and I recognized the need to defend myself. It isn't much, but it has gotten me out of a few sticky situations."

He clapped and rubbed his hands together. "Excellent. Since you're already comfortable with a blade, I'll teach you to knife fight. At least the basics."

I slid the cloak from my shoulders and tossed it to the side on the grass. Excitement shivered through me. I'd always longed to learn fighting skills.

An evil grin spread across Sky's lips. "I will not take it easy on you."

"Good."

Two hours later, I hobbled into the house, sore in places I didn't even know I could ache. Saber greeted me at the door.

"I ran you a bath. Saw you out there training and thought your might need it."

I almost melted right into a puddle of goo right there on the floor. Why was he so thoughtful and sweet? It made it really difficult to fear or dislike him. It made it almost impossible to continue keeping my emotional distance.

"Thanks. He wasn't kidding when he said he wouldn't take it easy on me."

Saber chuckled. "He loves training. It's what he did before we were chosen as assassins. He's also the best at hand to hand and daggers, so he was the perfect teacher for you."

"What are you and Whistler best at?"

"I'm best with swords and Whist prefers poisons."

"That makes perfect sense." Between Saber's name and Whist's love of gardens and cooking, their skills match them completely.

Saber held the washroom door open for me. "Do you need any help?"

Red spread from my cheeks and down my chest. "I-I'm good. Thanks."

He inclined his head. "Of course, love. Take your time." He closed the door behind him.

Steam rose from the surface of the water. Saber had even sprinkled lavender in the bath and the washroom flickered with candlelight. Dammit. What was I supposed to do with such thoughtfulness?

With only a couple winces and smothered yelps, I stripped off my clothes and climbed in the water. I hissed as I sank into it, the heat almost too much.

A moan slipped from my throat and I leaned against the back of the tub, the scent of lavender teasing my nose. The tension bled from my stiff muscles and I sighed in delight. Regular hot baths might have been the best reason to stay with the assassins. Such luxury was unheard of for me. I had the occasional lukewarm bath in the dead of winter when I was forced into inns and way-houses by the bitter elements.

I had a safe house of sorts of my own, but it didn't have plumbing. By the time I heated enough water for a bath, it was cold again. My safe house was more a shack than a house. It was one room with a chimney and a mattress on the floor. But it kept me alive during the winter and no one alive had any idea where it was.

And it would stay that way.

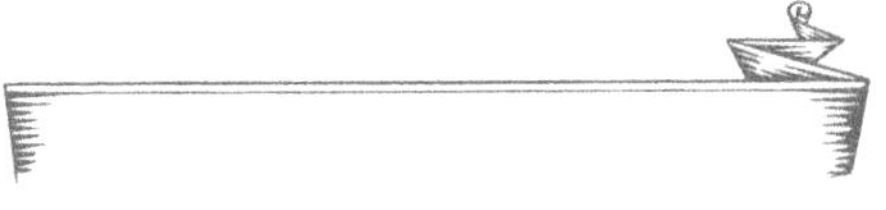

TWELVE

After another scrumptious meal made by Whist, I wandered over to the sofa and sat. I considered closing myself away from the assassins in the room they assigned me, but I'd been on my own so long, my soul craved companionship. Being a traveling bard was a lonely life. There was no way to keep in touch with people, especially since most people wanted nothing to do with me out of fear or disgust.

And the three men fascinated me. The way they moved and worked together, constantly aware of one another, a bond so tight they hardly needed words. I guessed it made sense they shared a kindred. If they didn't, they'd be torn apart, headed for separate lives and that would be a shame.

Saber slipped out of my room with my ukulele in his hands. I hadn't even noticed him leave the main room. Sneaky bastard. "Here." He handed me my instrument. "Play."

I stared at him with wide eyes. "What?"

"We've never really heard you. We've heard you quoted and a little of your music trickled from the tavern the other day, but we want to see you perform. Well, Whist got to see you, but Sky and I didn't."

"Why?" I asked.

Sky rolled his eyes with a snort and a smirk. "Stop stalling and play, doll. You know exactly why we want to hear you. Don't be coy."

I shot Sky a glare, but I accepted my ukulele from Saber, gifting him with a smile.

Sky snorted again, but I ignored him.

Their expectant eyes burning into me made me fidget. I wasn't usually a nervous performer, but there was something bigger there. A part of me cared what they thought. Way too large a part of me.

I cleared my throat and closed my eyes, finding that place inside me. The still, quiet place—my safe place. Everything else fell away, my past, my worries, my fears, my bitterness. It was just me and the music, me and my lyrics.

My fingers plucked the strings, playing and searching for the right tune. Faster and faster, my fingers tripped and flew across the strings, my voice whispering from me, husky and low. When I reached the chorus, I sang louder, completely forgetting I had an audience, forgetting where I was. The only thing I was aware of was the music as it swept me away in its arms.

I moved into a softer tune, one I'd never played for anyone before, one I still hadn't written lyrics for. The words hadn't yet come to me, the music some of the best I'd done. I opened my eyes and met Saber's. His had tears pooling in the bottom and his expression was filled with awe.

Sky stood from his chair and pulled Saber to his feet, drawing him close. They moved fluidly in a dance. My chest tightened as I watched, mesmerized. They were beautiful together, light and dark pushing, pulling, melding together. I glanced over at Whist where he watched from the shadows, his eyes glittering like stars in the black sky.

Candlelight flickered around us, the only light in the darkness, making it all the more intimate. Sky had a serious expression on his face for once as he gazed into Saber's eyes. What was between them? It was something more than mere friendship or brotherhood. Whatever it was, it scorched me.

I replayed the song, not wanting the moment to end, wanting to draw it out. Sky and Saber moved even closer, their bodies pressed together. They were similar in height, Saber an inch or so taller, Sky a little bit broader. Dark fingers tangled in pale. My stomach fluttered, and I was barely able to focus on my music. I could have watched them forever.

Heat sank into me from behind and Whist bent over to whisper in my ear, his breath teasing my neck. "They're performing for you, gorgeous."

I shivered, but kept playing. I finally knew what Whist's scent was. He smelled of winter nights and herbs, something clear, dark, and fresh.

"Do you like the idea of the two of them? Aren't they beautiful? Does it turn you on to see them pressed so close? They've been waiting for you for a long time, but they still love each other. Part of them was terrified they'd be ripped apart when they found their kindreds. Do you have any idea how relieved they are they share one? And that you don't seem the type who will be jealous and try to keep them apart. That you believe in having a choice in who you love? They chose each other a long time ago and as much as they crave the kindred connection, they don't want to lose what they have." Whist kept his voice low, his lips brushing my skin.

I swallowed the lump in my throat, desire and sadness at war within me. Desire to join them, sadness for their fear—a common story in our world. I'd seen the beauty between kindreds, the completion and peace they could bring each other. But I'd seen the other side too. When their connection warped into obsession. The damage they caused each other.

As much as I railed against kindreds, I didn't actually wish whatever magic it was didn't exist. I just never thought I'd find my own. I wasn't born to kindreds. I'd never heard of someone like me finding one. Granted, there weren't many people like me. Non-kindreds were careful not to get pregnant, using herbs to prevent any accidents like me.

We weren't supposed to get our happy endings. Not that I believed in them, anyway.

Saber pressed a soft kiss to Sky's collarbone. I could almost feel the touch of his lips on my skin.

"You're what we've been searching for, gorgeous. Can't you feel it? The rightness between us? We're fated. Why would you fight it?" Whist didn't touch me, but his proximity raised the hair along my spine.

My fingers faltered, and I played the wrong note with a discordant twang.

THIRTEEN

Saber and Sky broke apart and Whist returned to the shadows.

"Sorry." My breath came too fast and my face flushed with heat.

"No problem, love. Your music is gorgeous." Saber fell back onto the sofa, pulling a laughing Sky beside him.

"Thanks." I ducked my head, uncomfortable with their praise.

Sky sat forward. "He's right. It's a shame your talent is only garnering you a few coins and the occasional free meal. You'd be flush if you came to the palace."

A harsh laugh fell from my lips. "I have absolutely zero interest in playing for royals. Besides, I don't do this for money. And I get by just fine."

"Too bad, though. I wish we could bring you to our place in the capital instead of sticking you in this hovel." Sky sniffed and cast a glance of distaste around the room.

"Hovel? What?" This is a castle compared to the places I've lived.

Whist sat on the edge of my chair. "Ignore him. Sky has a love of all things lavish in life. He's a spoiled brat."

"So what if I like nice things? I can afford them." Sky sat back and crossed his arms with a fake pout.

Whist grunted. "Yes, and you fill our home to the brim with things we don't need and we're rarely there to enjoy."

Sky tossed his hands into the air. "Have you forgotten the elaborate kitchen I had decorated and perfected for you? You weren't so grumpy over your new and shiny cooking toys."

I grinned as I watched their back and forth, bickering like brothers. It was a shame they had to leave their home and the people they cared about behind.

Because of me.

But it was their choice. Even with the connection riding us, it was still possible to say no to the bond. Especially before it was solidified. They chose to protect and remain with me. Even though Saber and Sky already had each other.

They made a choice. Now, I had to make mine.

Problem was, I still had no idea which one to make.

After spending the day with them, getting to know them, I was more intrigued than ever. More tempted. To stay, to see where this led us. If it led to love, to family.

But there were things I'd have to sacrifice to be with them. And as charming as they were, I didn't know if they were worth it. As near perfect as Whist's earlier words were, I didn't wholly believe them. I didn't dare.

Saber handed me a glass of brandy with a soft smile, his eyes seeming to reach through me and pluck the thoughts right from my head. I sniffed the amber liquid swirling in the glass and my heart clenched.

My favorite brand.

FOURTEEN

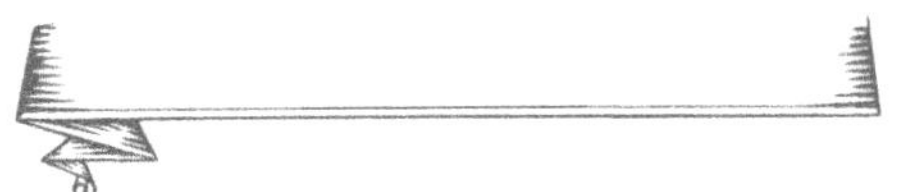

After drinking and chatting long into the night, I finally headed for bed. I didn't talk much, letting them regale me with their adventures as young soldiers. They didn't speak much of their lives as assassins. I was beginning to believe they hated it. They had no choice in their career and I could understand balking against it. I understood straining against the rules, the box you're forced into.

I grabbed a glass of water to take to bed with me and when I turned around; I was alone except for Sky. He cornered me against the counter, no sign of a smirk of humor. My heart thudded in my chest at the pure want on his face.

He took the glass from my shaking hands and set it on the counter. "Did you enjoy watching Saber and me together?"

"I... it... yes." The confession breathed from my lips. I couldn't lie with him staring at me like that.

He stepped closer, his scent sinking into me. "Would you want to see us go further? Did you imagine it? Us writhing together, naked? Did it make you wet? I know it made your nipples hard. I saw it."

I stopped breathing, caught in his gaze, lost in his deep voice saying filthy things.

His blue eyes blazed at me. "I can feel your nipples digging into my chest, begging me to taste them. I bet if I slid my hand into your pants, you'll be soaked for me."

I bit back a pathetic whimper. I didn't know what to think, what to do with this Sky. He was intense and domineering, the flirtatious, charming side of him nowhere in sight.

He traced a finger down the side of my face. "Would you want Whist to take you while you watch me take Saber? Or would you rather be in between us as Saber and I take you at the same time while Whist watches? Whist likes to watch, you know. He watches us all the time. It's partly what makes him so good at his job."

I shuddered and breathed out a shaky sigh.

I wanted either, both. I wanted it all.

"Turn around and place your hands on the counter." His tone brooked no argument even if I wanted to, it brimmed with a deep command that expected obedience.

So, I obeyed.

Sky's body trapped me from the back, his hands coming down to rest on top of mine, pinning me to the counter. "Do you want this?"

I gasped as his hips ground into my ass.

"Answer me." He didn't touch me in any other way, waiting for my response.

I did. I wanted it more than anything. Getting to know them all day, enjoying their company, coming alive beneath each touch and smile, it all led to this. "Yes."

His breathing hitched. "Good. I won't stop unless you tell me to. Do you understand?"

"Y-yes." I arched back against him, giving in to the desire riding me. I didn't know if it was the bond or if it was just the magnetic pull of Sky or if I'd just been alone for way too long and I crave touch, release. But in the moment, I didn't give the slightest fuck.

He released me and pulled back a little. "Do not move your hands from this spot."

I nodded, frantic, desperate.

He cupped my hips, pressing harder into me. He was as hard as a stone and large. My mouth watered. His hands slid up my sides, over my ribs, and past my breasts to my neck, teasing me. I made a small sound of distress, causing him to release a dark chuckle in my ear.

"Patience, doll."

One of his legs slipped between mine and he kicked at my feet, widening my stance, opening me up. He played with the hem of my woven shirt, his fingers brushing against the skin of my belly.

Finally, finally, he plunged his hands up my shirt, grabbing my breasts, plucking my nipples and rolling them between his fingers. He used his grip on them to clutch me tighter. I gasped and moaned, wordlessly begging for more, more, more.

He obliged.

Sky's hand dove beneath the waistband of my trousers, straight to the core of me. "Fuck, I knew you'd be wet. You want us, don't you, doll? You want to be screaming between us as we fuck you until you can't move."

My knees almost buckled, but his other hand kept me steady against him.

He flicked my clit, making me buck against his hand. "Remember what I said. Do not move your hands."

I found my voice. "Or what?"

"Or you'll be punished." His words were a dark promise, sending a shivery thrill through me.

I wanted to ask how he'd punish me, but his fingers sped up against my clit and then he shoved two deep inside me. I cried out and clenched hard on his fingers.

"Shit, you're so hot and tight. I bet you taste just like you smell. Like autumn trees and dahlias and forbidden music." He slid his fingers in and out of me while his other hand continued torturing my breast.

Everything he was doing brought me closer and closer to the edge, but never quite over it and I wanted more, more, more.

I wanted him to rip the clothes from my body and then his own, and plunge inside me, taking me right there against the counter.

Instead, he added a third finger inside me, stretching me, and sped up his thrusts until he fucked me hard with his hand. I was a panting and mewling mess, gripping the edge of the counter and leaning against him.

Something flickered from the corner of my eye and when I turned my head, I saw Whist. He was in the corner, watching. My eyes met his, and that's all it took to send me careening over the edge. I cried out and shuddered while Sky rode me through it, not letting up, making my climax linger.

He pulled out of me and spun me around, making sure I was looking at him as he raised his hand to his mouth and sucked on his fingers with closed eyes and a groan. I whimpered at the sight, wet and aching for him all over again.

My back dug into the counter as I stared at him, still shaky and wobbly-kneed, my mind cloudy with confusion.

Sky stepped back, putting way too much distance between us. "Go to bed, doll. Now. Or I won't be responsible for what I do to you next."

I listened, fleeing past Whist and his burning eyes and slammed the bedroom door behind me. I leaned against it, breathing hard.

What the fuck had I just done?

FIFTEEN

Nerves kept me staring at the door for far too long the following morning. My sleep had been restless as I tossed about, one minute wishing I wasn't alone, the next wishing I'd told Sky no and gone right to my room.

Worried about how they were going to act, what they'd say, I almost went back to bed. Instead, I sucked it up and swept through the door with my head held high, refusing to show shame.

Besides, I could smell bacon.

When I emerged, the assassins glanced up at me and welcomed me with smiles. Smiles a little too innocent, but I preferred it to winks and nudges and knowing looks. I'd seen men act like that in taverns and it always pissed me right off.

Nice to know my kindreds were of a better breed.

I slid into the free seat between Saber and Whist. "Morning."

A chorus of greetings came from the assassins.

Whist made me a plate and set it in front of me. "Eat."

"Thanks. Looks great." I avoided eye contact and fidgeted in my seat.

Saber's hand brushed my back. "He's really been upping his game since we brought you here."

Nervous laughter bubbled up my throat. "Oh yeah? Trying to convince me to stick around?" I wouldn't admit, it was working the slightest bit. Who knew I could be bought with hot baths and hot meals and hot men?

"Perhaps. Is it working, gorgeous?" Whist sat with his own plate of food.

I tried to play it off, focusing on my food instead of him. "Maybe a little. You still haven't figured out my favorite though."

Whist's eyes gleamed with the challenge. "Care to make a wager?"

My fork paused halfway to my mouth. "What sort of wager?"

A wicked smile unfurled on his lips. "If I can figure it out and make it as good as you remember, you stay with us for at least three weeks."

Sky laughed and rubbed his hands together.

"And if you don't?" There was no way. Everyone who ever knew my favorite was dead, and I hadn't eaten it since.

"What do you want?" Whist tilted his head as he studied me.

I opened my mouth to tell him to agree to let me go, but something inside me snapped it closed. "I'll let you know once you fail."

Whist grinned at me. "Deal."

I narrowed my eyes at him. "I look forward to knocking that cocky smirk off your face."

"We'll see, gorgeous."

I smiled and tucked into the food, confident he'd never guess treacle tarts. They were no longer a popular dessert. Hadn't been for years since I was a child. I was also looking forward to all the yummy treats he'd be making to try to guess.

Whist was making up for years of borderline starvation.

Sky pushed his empty plate across the table. "Want another knife lesson after breakfast?"

Still sore from the day before, I took a moment to consider. I also wasn't sure if I wanted to be in such proximity to him now that I knew what his hands could do to me. "I might need an hour to digest this, but sure."

"Is she any good?" Whist asked.

Sky nodded. "She's still rusty, but she's a quick learner. And she's damn handy with a knife. Worries too much about her hands though."

I polished the last bit of eggs off my plate. "I'm sitting right here, jackasses. And I'm careful with my hands because I won't be able to play if I damage them."

Whist frowned in disapproval. "You won't be able to play if someone slits your throat either. Broken hands heal."

"I promise if someone actually attacks me I won't hold back. But in training, I will not take the chance."

Whist huffed, but didn't argue farther.

SIXTEEN

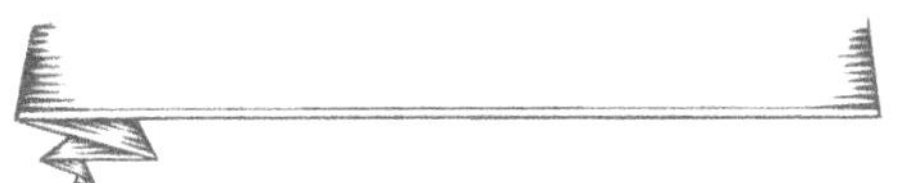

The bloody assassins had me so completely turned on and trembly by dinnertime, I could barely eat. Even then, they wouldn't cut me a break, their legs sliding against mine, their eyes on fire with desire scorched me as they roamed up and down my body. The whispered words passed back and forth between Saber and Sky reminded me of them tangled together in a dance.

The day was spent much like the one before—gardening with Whist, training with Sky, a bath prepared for me by Saber and afterward a long conversation about music and art. The man had deep layers I kept peeling away and discovering something new. It was like they were trying to get to know me and for me to know them. And their seemingly innocent touches had me doused in flames.

"I want to head out tomorrow and see what's going on." Whist's words doused the fire.

Sky and Saber didn't appear the slightest bit surprised.

My fork clattered against my plate. "What's going on with what?"

Whist gestured at me with his cup of wine. "With you. With us. I want to know how serious they are about tracking us down, or if they're satisfied as long as you aren't performing and they think we've shut you up."

"How are you planning to determine that? Capture a guard and interrogate them?"

Whist shook his head with a snort. "Nothing so sinister. I'm going to go to the nearest town and listen. See what gossip people are spreading and see how big the show of force is. If they're still determined to find us, they'll be in the towns closest to the village we rescued you from."

I scowled. "You didn't rescue me. I decided to go along with you after I escaped on my own."

"Whatever you say, gorgeous." A small smile played on his lips.

"And I'm going with you." I needed to get out of this house and clear my head. Even if I still had to be around one of them. Playing house was muddling my thoughts and making it impossible for me to make a rational decision.

Whist slammed his cup onto the table. "Absolutely not."

Saber and Sky were quick to add their disagreement.

I met Whist's angry gaze with a stubborn jaw. "Yes. I am."

"Why? We can't afford for you to perform right now. It's too risky. For all of us, not just you."

"It's perfect. I can draw them out." I sipped my brandy calmly, hiding my desperation.

"I don't need you to draw them out. We don't want to poke the bear. The goal is for them to back off and leave us alone. If you throw yourself in the king's face after stealing away his three best assassins, he'll come after you with everything he has. The king is a bit bored. He's already begun passing stupid laws to try to rustle up drama. The last thing we want is for you to become his new project." Whist shoved back from the table and ran fingers through his red hair.

I had to convince him. He said they wouldn't take away my choices or stop me from playing. He had to understand he wasn't my commanding officer. He didn't get to tell me what to do. "What if I only perform popular songs? At least then we'll know if he has the guard pulling in all the traveling bards or they know what I look like. Which would be worrisome because I change my appearance pretty regularly."

"That wasn't in your file." Saber sounded almost offended.

I snorted. "Based on what you seemed to know about me, my file was pretty thin."

Saber still seemed annoyed. "True."

Why was he so bothered? It was a good thing the king and the guard and the other assassins knew so little about me.

Sky tapped his lips with his finger. "It might not be the worst idea. We can protect her and we do need to know as much as possible. We're blind out here."

Whist shook his head. "It's too dangerous for all of us to go. They're looking for her and three men."

Sky drained his drink and set it on the table. "Then Saber and I stay here and if you two aren't back by nightfall, we'll set out to your rescue."

Whist growled and gripped the back of his vacant chair. "I do not like this plan. It's foolhardy and dangerous."

"Too bad." I shrugged and shot him a challenging look.

Whist glared at me, his knuckles whitening. "I have conditions or I'll tie your pretty ass up and leave you here."

Of course he did. Blasted man couldn't stand not being in control. "What are they?"

"You will not perform if it's obvious guards are everywhere searching for us."

Fair enough. I didn't actually want to be arrested and then executed. "Fine."

"I'm not done. You will also do whatever I tell you when I tell you. I'm not just trying to keep you safe, it's for the rest of us as well." His gaze softened the slightest bit, giving me a peek at the pleading lurking in his eyes.

In the moment, I completely understood him. He wanted to give me what I wanted, but it warred with his desire to keep me and the others safe. He was honoring his words to me, but it was going against every instinct he had.

Damn, he was a man I could easily love. Even without the bond.

"All right." I peeled my eyes away from him and watched the brandy swirl in my glass.

"No political songs, no matter how much you're tempted. I admit I am curious if the king has ordered all the bards to be brought to him. I want to know how much he wants you. If there's already a performer in the town we go to, we just watch. And last, we both are going disguised and keep your ukulele hidden in your pack." Whist wasn't asking me for anything I wasn't willing to give. He was more than meeting me halfway.

"Agreed." I tried not to smile, not wanting him to think I was gloating. It was hard when I noticed Sky and Saber's wide-eyed surprise.

Whist stepped forward until he loomed above me. "I mean it, gorgeous. You must obey me every step of the way." Something in his eyes made me think he wasn't just talking about our little trip. Something that made my insides tremble with excitement.

SEVENTEEN

I forgot to knock on the bathroom door and instead barged right in on Saber stepping out of the bath and was treated to a full eyeful. Of everything.

My mouth gaped as my eyes roamed up and down his brown, glistening body. Rippling muscles covered his chest and arms, marred by the occasional scar, but it made him hotter. His cock grew even larger under my gaze. My wide eyes rose to meet his, and he was watching me with a rare glint of amusement mingling with the heat in his expression.

"S-sorry. I should have knocked."

"That's all right, love. There's nothing I want to hide from you."

I nodded so hard my teeth snapped together. "Right. Right. Of course."

He grabbed a towel and wrapped it around his waist and I breathed a little easier even while a small pang of disappointment shot through me.

"Didn't you have a bath this morning after training with Sky?" He still had signs of amusement crinkling the corners of his fathomless eyes.

Like he forgot. He was the one who prepared it for me.

"I did. I came in to brush my teeth."

"By all means." He gestured to the sink where my brush and paste had joined theirs.

We shared a space over the sink while we freshened up, the smell of mint overpowering up the scent of his soap. Our arms kept brushing against each other, raising goosebumps along my skin.

Awkwardness filled me as we finished up and turned to return to our own rooms. Part of me wanted to draw it out, part of me wanted to run away, the largest part of me wanted to grab him and drag him into my room and into my bed.

The largest part of me won.

I stepped in close to him, eying the droplets of water trickling down his chest. I wanted to lick each one off his skin.

"Stop looking at me like that, love. I don't know if you're ready for what it will mean if you don't." His voice came out deep and rumbling.

I tilted my head and placed my hands on his chest. "I'm ready."

He peered at me and searched my face. "Are you sure?"

"Yes." And I was. So sure. So ready.

"Good." He kissed me softly, barely a peck before sweeping me up off of my feet and into his arms like he was some hero from a story. I refused to acknowledge even to myself how hard it made me swoon.

Saber carried me into my bedroom and laid me with heart-breaking tenderness on the bed, then laid beside me on his side, hovering over me, staring down at me.

"I'm going to ask one last time if you're sure you're ready. I'm not going to stop like Sky did last night. I won't stop until I have you."

I gulped, trying to consider seriously. But my entire self—body and soul, screamed out at me how much I wanted him. My brain might have disagreed, but I couldn't hear it over the longing inside me.

"I don't want you to stop."

I didn't know if this was what they planned as they teased me all day or if they just couldn't help themselves, and right then I didn't give a shit. They hadn't pressured me or tried to force me or even manipulate me. And it didn't mean I was in love or had decided to stay.

But perhaps I was one step closer to making that choice.

With a groan, Saber covered my upper body with his and took my lips in a kiss brimming with hunger. He was gentle, but still firm, demanding I open to him. His tongue slid inside my mouth, flirting with mine, drawing me into a teasing dance. I sighed into his mouth and wrapped my arms around his shoulders, pulling him closer. My hands slid down his back until I reached the towel and I yanked it off him.

Saber kissed me harder, his hands roving along my sides, but keeping his touch innocent. I squirmed beneath him and grabbed at his ass, squeezing with needy fingers.

He chuckled against my lips and pulled back so he could trail kisses across my cheeks, down my neck and down, down, down as he unbuttoned my shirt. Baring my breasts to his view, he hissed out a breath before falling on my left one with tongue and teeth.

I arched against him with a desperate moan. He continued his journey down my body with his mouth all the way to my waistband. With a few flicks of his tongue, he teased me until I writhed and grasped at the blankets beneath me. He slid my trousers off my legs, taking my underwear along with them and we were both naked.

He was so fucking gorgeous. I wanted to explore every inch of him.

My legs fell open, and he scooted down my body until he could bury his face in my core. I almost leapt from the bed. No one had ever done this to me. I'd heard about it whispered in the back of taverns and read about it in books, but most of my encounters were of the quick, one night varieties.

Saber grabbed my hips to keep me still as he pressed kisses on the inside of my thighs, opening me up even wider. He swept a long, hard lick right up the center of me before returning to nibble at the juncture of my thighs. The whimpering sigh escaping me was embarrassing, but I was too far gone to really care.

Every single nerve ending on my body buzzed with life and need and want.

He released my hips and spread my lower lips so he could suck and flick at my bud. I dug the heels of my palms into my eyes, trying to stay quiet, trying to stay still.

Candlelight danced across his skin making it glow. The muscles in his back and shoulders rippled as he continued pleasuring me.

Saber licked me harder and faster and slid two fingers inside me. I panted and trembled, a sheen of sweat rising on my skin. He fucked me with his fingers and teased me with his tongue until I was a mad mess, desperate and aching.

"I need you, Saber. Please." I needed him inside me, I needed to be filled with him, surrounded by him, pressed down by his weight.

He raised his head from my pussy, but didn't slow the thrust of his fingers. "I'm right here, love. Trust me to take care of you."

I nodded frantically. Anything he wanted to bring me back to the edge.

He smiled. "Sky told me you tasted like heaven, but I didn't realize how right he was. I can't get enough of you."

All I could do was whimper again in response. His eyes flared, and he dove back into my pussy, his tongue lashings messier, wilder. He kept making little sounds of enjoyment and bliss, his free hand reaching up and play with my nipple.

My breathing quickened and the heat in my belly boiled over and my entire body locked tight. I grabbed the pillow and stuffed it over my face to muffle my scream and I shook and bucked.

Saber gave me one last lingering lick and crawled back up my body, removing the pillow from my face to smile at me.

EIGHTEEN

Never in my life had I climaxed so hard. I wasn't sure if it was his skill or because he was my kindred. He covered my body with his and pressed his lips to mine.

He brushed strands of hair from my face. "You're beautiful when you come, love. Don't hide your face from me."

Still panting, I kissed him quickly. "I wasn't hiding, I was muffling my screams."

"Definitely don't hide those. I want the others to know how well I'm treating you." He nibbled at my jawline.

"I didn't want to wake them." My breaths still came in pants and gasps.

He chuckled softly. "Oh, love. They're not asleep."

They were listening? I hadn't considered that. "Well, then I didn't want them to come bursting inside."

"Why? You don't want them to join us?" He dropped a kiss on my collarbone, the same spot his kissed Sky the other night.

My mind went blank as I imagined it. Me, with the three of them. It excited me and terrified me all at the same time. "I might need to work my way up to that."

"Fair enough."

I enjoyed his weight on mine, but I wanted more. I squirmed to hint at my renewed interest.

A smile quirked the edges of his lips. "Don't worry. I'm nowhere near finished with you yet."

I shivered and trailed my hands idly across his back. "Good."

"I told you I would not stop. After tasting you, I'm not sure I ever can." He rolled us over to the middle of the bed, settling me on top of him so I straddled his waist.

Saber grabbed me by the back of the neck and pulled my lips to his, his hard cock twitching against me. I ground against him, making him groan. Already wet and aching again, I lifted up and grabbed him, stroking him up and down. His eyes squeezed shut and his hips rose. I aimed his cock at the right position and I slid down on him, slowly since I'd never had anyone as big as him. He stretched me to my limits, stole my breath. It hurt a bit, but it quickly morphed into pure pleasure.

Saber remained still, giving me control, letting me set the pace, his teeth gritted against his need to thrust against me. When he reached the hilt, buried deep inside me, my head dropped and my eyes rolled back in ecstasy. Nothing had ever felt so good, so right.

Saber let out a string of muttered curses. "Fuck, love. You feel even better than you tasted. Take your time. Take what you need."

My heart melted at his words. No one had ever cared whether I got off or not. No one ever gave me control like this before. How did he do it? Know what I needed. Know what I wanted.

I circled my hips and drew him even deeper inside me. I grasped his shoulders, and he grabbed my ass to keep me steady as I worked him in and out of me, faster and faster, harder and harder, until we were both breathless and sweaty.

I leaned down and plastered myself against him as I kept pumping my hips. His fingers dug into the flesh of my ass as he met my thrusts with his own. Tension knotted in my stomach, winding tighter and tighter and I flew higher and higher.

Our grunts and moans created a sultry harmony, rising in a crescendo as we neared release. I clutched his shoulders harder, my nails sinking into skin.

I came first, singing out my climax into his mouth. Once my pussy grasped and clenched at him, he was right behind me.

With a gasp, I collapsed against him and rested my head on his shoulder, fighting to get my breath back. Saber's hands trailed along my back with lazy strokes.

"You're amazing, love."

I huffed a laugh into his skin. "Can't say I have any complaints either."

He kissed the top of my head. "Can I stay in here with you tonight?"

"Won't Sky miss you?" I'd assumed Saber would head back to Sky.

Saber chuckled and hugged me to him. "It's not like that. He'll be jealous I got to spend the night with you, but he won't be upset I'm with you instead of with him."

"I don't want to come between you." The thought made my stomach hurt.

"You won't. You'll just join us."

I kept my face hidden in the crook of his shoulder. "Whist mentioned you and Sky were worried about being separated when you found your kindred."

Saber rolled me off of him and curled me into his side, yanking the blankets over us. "We were. We wanted desperately to find you, but we always assumed we'd have different kindreds. It would change things between us because we would never be unfaithful.

And then when we found you and realized we share you, there was still the fear it would cause problems. Some multiple pairings get awkward with jealousies and backstabbing. But you, love. You didn't have the slightest jealousy when you saw Sky and I dance. In fact, you liked it. You're the answer to every hope we've ever had. For all three of us."

"Even though now you've lost your jobs and are on the run from the king?" Perhaps Whist had come to terms with it, but Saber and Sky must have had people they wanted to see again.

"We hate our jobs, love. It's no sacrifice. And we'll figure out a way to work everything else out. Don't worry. Even your determination to continue railing against the royals."

"But how?" Whist had his plans and ideas, but would they really work? I was terrified I'd get one or all of them killed.

"I don't know yet. We need more information which is what you and Whist are going to do tomorrow. From there, hopefully we'll have an idea of our next move." He kissed the top of my head again. It's like he couldn't help himself, couldn't stop touching me, kissing me, holding me tight.

"I'm surprised he agreed." I had a hard time focusing on our conversation instead of basking in the afterglow. My body had never been so relaxed. I'd never felt so at ease and fulfilled. I could get used to the feeling.

"He's a bit of a... well, he's stern and dominant and wants his own way, but he's not controlling. He will never try to force you into anything you don't want to do. And he won't stop you from doing what you do want to do. He'll try to talk you out of it. Strenuously. But he'll respect your choices."

Choice. Is that what kindreds really were? Perfect matches? The missing pieces? I always heard it described as such, but I never really believed it or understood its power.

I was starting to believe kindreds could be a true gift. One I wasn't prepared to walk away from.

With Saber's continued strokes up and down my back, his scent lulling me, sleep came for me on swift feet.

NINETEEN

Sky and Saber watched Whist and I with worry darkening their eyes.

I smiled and patted Saber on the arm. "We'll be fine. I'll make sure Whist doesn't get into any trouble."

A growl rumbled from Whist while Sky laughed and Saber pulled me into a gentle hug. "You have until nightfall and we're coming after you."

"Better make it morning." Whist adjusted the pack on his back.

"Morning, eh?" Sky smirked and wagged his eyebrows.

Whist rolled his eyes. "She wants to perform. It'll take us three hours there, three hours back, at least a couple hours spent in town. I doubt we can make it back before tonight. Don't worry until morning."

Sky sobers. "Fine. But try to make it back anyway. We won't get any sleep with the two of you out there with no backup."

I shouldered my pack and shot Sky a cheeky smile. "I'm sure the two of you can figure out a way to pass the time."

Sky laughed and swatted me on the ass. "Brat."

Whist held the door open for me. "Come on. We should have left an hour ago."

Like it was my fault, the plonker. "You were the one who insisted on a big breakfast. And you still haven't guessed it, by the way."

"I will." Whist's tone was harsh with grim determination.

I wrinkled my nose at him. "Whatever you say."

Whist shook his head and took the lead through the woods. He set a brisk pace, but not too quick for me to keep up. A companionable silence fell over us, comfortable instead of awkward. Whist had a restful way about him, not very talkative, which set me at ease. There was a lot on my mind I needed to sort through.

After about an hour, Whist called a halt. "Let's take a break for a minute."

"Tired already?" I was relieved. My body still pulsed with soreness from training with Sky and my night with Saber.

He drank deeply from his metal bottle of water. "Sky was right. You are a brat."

"Yep." I studied our surroundings, trying to determine where we were. With him in the lead I hadn't paid attention to our location, just followed, lost in thought. I didn't recognize it, but it looked like most of the forests. Lots of trees with changing colors. Lots of scraggly bushes. Lots of dead leaves.

Whist snorted and handed me the bottle. "Afraid it's not brandy."

"I'll make do." Brandy sounded delicious though.

He subsided back into silence, a mask over his face. Something in me desperately wanted to smash his mask and read everything beneath it. He had let me in for a moment in the garden that first day, but I'd glimpsed only flashes since. The others, I felt like I understood and even knew to the extent I could after only knowing them a couple days. But Whistler was an enigma. Even Saber's mysterious air I found a way through.

"Why are you so passionate about cooking?"

Surprise peeked through his facade for a moment before he wiped it clean. "My mother. Sky told you she works as the chef in the palace kitchens. She taught me when I was young and we learned I have a gift for it." He shrugged. "Comes in handy with my job. Easy to slip poisons inside food. I know how to hide the taste."

"That's not terrifying at all." I shuddered and handed the bottle back to him.

He gifted me with a rare grin that sent my heart into palpitations. I'd never seen anything so beautiful as his smile. It completely transformed his face, softening the harsh angles, lightening the dark violence in his eyes.

His smile melded into a frown. "What?"

"What?" I cleared my throat and turned my attention to my feet instead of him.

"Why were you looking at me like that?"

"Like what?" I played dumb, not at all interested in explaining. He'd probably never smile again if I told him.

"Like... nevermind." He huffed. "We need to get moving."

I smothered a grin and followed him back towards the trail.

We reached the edge of Harpot right before midday. Whist dug around in his pack and pulled out a fancy embroidered dress and handed it to me.

I frowned at it with distaste. "What is this for?"

He shook it at me. "I told you we needed to be in disguise. Apparently, you never wear dresses."

Apparently my file wasn't quite as thin as I'd hoped. "Because they're uncomfortable and make it difficult to run when people are chasing you."

"No one will be chasing you today. You need to do something different with your hair as well."

I tug on the end of my usual braid. "Any suggestions? I'm not great at fixing hair."

"I'll take care of it when I get back."

"Where are you going?" I took the dress from him with a wrinkled nose.

"I'm going to do a quick recon of the village and see what's going on."

"You're not in disguise. If there are guards, won't they recognize you?" I was oddly reluctant to part from him.

He pulled out a black hooded cape. "I'm an assassin. I know how to be invisible. I'll change into something else when I return." He didn't give me a chance to argue further, instead he proved his words by fading away into the trees.

With a sigh, I stripped off my cloak and shirt and yanked the dress over my head. It was a forest green, the same shade as my eyes and my usual cloak, with fancy gold stitching. It was pretty, but already my ribs felt crushed and it was harder to breathe.

Music was my life, I hated anything constricting my breathing. My breasts were all but falling from the bodice no matter how much I tried to stuff them inside. Whoever the dress belonged to was a wee bit smaller than me.

I left my trousers and my boots on. The dress hid any sign, and it kept my legs warm. Women's clothing made no sense to me. My cold fingers unraveled my braid, combing out the tangles in my dark wavy hair.

A snapping twig at my back spun me around to find Whist standing there. "How do you do that?"

"Training." His eyes widened as he took me in. "You definitely don't look like yourself."

"Not even a little." I scowled at my heaving bosom. Ridiculous. Why would anyone voluntarily wear something so awful?

"We were informed about your green cloak, so you can borrow my black one." He tossed it to me and stripped from his clothes.

"What about you?" I gathered my loose belongings and returned them to my pack, keeping my attention down, telling myself not to watch.

I took a quick peek, then breathed easier when I found him dressed. Whist had transformed from an assassin into a farmer. He had on tan trousers clinging to his muscular legs and a dark brown sweater. There was the man who belonged in a garden digging in the dirt.

"I'll be fine. You have goosebumps." He gestured at my chest.

I hefted my bad over my shoulder. "Do I want to know where you got this dress?"

"Probably not."

I snorted. 'Whoever she was, she had terrible taste."

"Agreed."

My brows shot high with surprise. "You don't like it?"

"You look gorgeous as always, but I prefer you in your usual clothes." He shrugged, like it wasn't a big deal. Like he hadn't just poured warmth right through me. "What?"

He had no idea, the gift he'd given me. "Nothing."

"All right. Let's move. Remember. What I say, you do." He certainly knew how to ruin a moment.

TWENTY

Harpot was a town I had yet to perform in, so I shouldn't be recognized. It looked like every other village in Faligrey, the markets were the same, the simple shops selling fabrics and hardware, the rows of homes, the wooden sidewalks and dirt roads. The villages closer to the palace were more elaborate, or so I'd heard. I'd been saving up money and planning to make the trip in the spring. Which was now a death warrant.

Whistler escorted me to one of the three taverns in Harpot. We chose seats in the back corner where we could see and hear everyone else, but as long as we were quiet, no one could hear us.

A server approached and smiled at us. "New in town?"

"Just visiting." Whist's eyes roved across the room.

"What can I get the two of you? We have a real nice steak and wild mushroom soup." The server gestured over his shoulder at the kitchen door.

Whist raised his brows at me in question and I nodded. "Sounds good. Two and some fresh bread and coffees, please."

"Right away." The server bustled away.

I leaned closer to Whist, stealing a quick sniff of his scent. "That's not my favorite either."

"As delicious as I hope it is, that would be a boring choice. I'm pretty certain it's a dessert. I noticed you seem to enjoy sweets." He didn't stop searching the crowd of diners.

I shrugged. "I don't get sweets very often. Most of my diet was tinned food before you."

Whist shuddered. "Never again as long as you stay with us."

"Trying to bribe me to stick around?" I asked it in a teasing tone, but I wondered if he was.

He met my eyes, utterly serious. "I'll do whatever I need to to convince you to choose us."

I gulped, tears clogging my throat. "I'll keep that in mind." My voice was raw and hoarse.

"Good." So was his.

The server returned, breaking up our moment, and I relaxed some while we turned our attention to the food. The soup was good, but I had been spoiled by Whistler. It wasn't as flavorful as his cooking, just hearty and plain and filling.

I still scraped up every drop while we perked our ears to listen to the other patrons. No one mentioned the royal guards, musicians, or the king. It was the usual gossip and complaints and pleasantries.

Whist leaned over in the booth so his words wouldn't be overheard. "Nothing. It seems like the guard hasn't come here looking for you. Which makes no sense. It's the second closest village to the one you performed in last time and they were crawling through that one. Why aren't they here?"

I agreed. It didn't make sense. "Maybe since I disappeared, they assumed I ran. Or went farther than the closest village?"

He didn't seem convinced. "Maybe. They still should have at least checked though."

"You're just grumpy because this means I get to perform. We'll know for sure then."

Resignation crossed his face. "Go ahead and ask. Let's get this over with."

Whist disappeared after the tavern owner agreed to let me play for the cost of our meal. I considered negotiating for a little coin as well, but it was more important I play than to tuck away a little more money in preparation for a rainy day.

Instead of using one of my extra instruments, I sat on a stool with nothing but my ukulele. Thankfully, it was a common instrument for musicians. Especially traveling ones because the small size made it easy to transport.

I made sure it was still in tune after its trip there and then plunged into a ballad, one not as popular as it used to be, but if I couldn't play what I really wanted, I could still play my mother's favorite song. She and Papa used to dance to this song after Papa taught it to me, laughing and kissing in the candlelight. It was one of my few bright memories of them before poverty and sickness turned everything gray.

I barely finished the song and moved into the next one before a couple royal guards walked in with their deep purple uniforms pressed and clean, their brass buttons shiny like new.

I made sure my eyes passed right over them, not showing the nervousness fluttering in my belly. Where had Whist run off to? The guards kept their eyes trained on me, but didn't approach, instead moving to take a seat and order some food.

A large part of me was tempted to play my treasonous songs, to sing it right in their faces. Rage at the king and his loyal lapdogs banished any hint of nerves. But Whistler was somewhere nearby and he'd be caught in the crossfire if I tried anything or tipped my hand.

And I was growing rather fond of the grumpy assassin and didn't want his death on my conscience.

Instead, I started another song, a more current one. The patrons sang along, joining their voices with mine. This was something I missed, something I rarely got to experience since I perform so many originals.

There was something powerful in so many voices raised together in harmony. If I could recreate this magic with one of my treasonous songs, we could change the world.

My hour of playing ended, and I slid off the stool to applause. That was new. And a little disconcerting. I'd never done this for acclamation, but I had to admit it was rather nice.

The tavern owner smiled and handed me a couple coins. Also new. Guessed he appreciated my efforts. And the money spent as people lingered over their meals.

Assuming Whist would find me once he was ready, I left the tavern. And the guards filed out after me.

TWENTY-ONE

More guards waited for me outside. In seconds, they surrounded me.

"Can I help you?" I blinked up at them, the picture of innocence.

"What's your name?" One of the guards from inside the tavern asked me.

"Dahlia." The name fell from my lips without thought as I remembered Saber's words from the night before. Seemed appropriate since I apparently smelled like the cool weather flower.

Another guard stepped up to his comrade's side. "Your occupation is a traveling bard?"

"It is. Has that become a crime?" I couldn't keep the question from tumbling from my mouth, but I tried to make it sound saucy.

The second guard took over the interrogation and the first one blended back with the others. "It depends. What sort of music do you play?"

Their questions were gathering a crowd as villagers slowed and craned their necks to watch.

I frowned in pretend confusion. "Weren't you inside? I play all sorts of music."

"But nothing seditious?"

This was getting ridiculous. Were they going to arrest me or just ask stupid questions? No wonder the king decided he needed assassins. His guards were idiots. "What would even be considered seditious? Faligrey has freedom of expression."

"Do you sing against kindred souls or the king?"

I gasped and clasped a hand to my chest. "Of course not. Why on earth would I sing against kindreds? Part of the reason I chose this occupation is to search for my kindred."

"You haven't found yours?" The guards were softening, and the one questioning me was sounding bored. How many times had they done this?

I shook my head sadly and forced a pout onto my lips. "No." I wished I knew where one of my kindreds was at the moment, but I was too scared to look for him in case it gave us away.

"Who was that man with you earlier?"

Shit, we should have considered having a better plan in place. "My brother." Hopefully, Whist hadn't been questioned and given different answers.

"Where is he now?"

I shrugged. "I don't know. I'm not his keeper. He travels with me in search of his own kindred and to keep me safe."

"So, you don't travel alone?" He stepped forward like he was trying to intimidate me.

"No." I shook my head. "It wouldn't be safe for me to travel all by myself with no one to protect me." I was probably laying it on a bit thick, but I was growing impatient.

"Have you heard of a bard named Rhapsody?"

I bobbed my head in an enthusiastic nod. "I've heard of her, but I've never met her."

"Are you sure?" The guard's eyes narrowed on me.

"Of course I'm sure. Our line of work tends to be pretty solitary. If another bard is in town, I move on. What is this about?" It was time to be a nosy, curious woman.

"Not important."

"Is she in some sort of trouble? Has she broken the law?" I pressed a hand to my chest again. Whoever I was pretending to be was ridiculous, and I had never seen a woman actually act like it, but they were lapping it up. Idiots.

He cleared his throat. "Like I said, it's not important. Or your business."

"All right. Can I go now? I need to track down my brother if we want to make it to the next village before nightfall." I glanced up at the sky like I was checking the time.

"You can go. It might be a good time to take a little time off." His words were dark with warning. It would probably be smart to listen.

"I'll keep that in mind. Have a nice rest of your day."

He gave me a sharp nod and turned on his heel, his comrades trailing in his wake. I waited until they turned the corner before I hurried towards the woods. I needed to get out of there as soon as possible.

I didn't stop until I made it twenty minutes away from the village, tripping through brush instead of staying on the trail. Dropping my pack, I stopped and bent over, hands on my knees, and panted for breath.

A body crashed into me and slammed me into a tree.

TWENTY-TWO

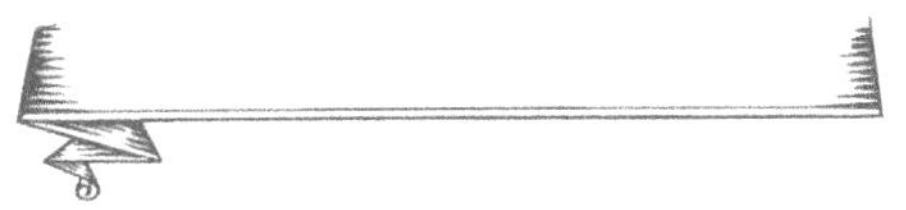

I struggled until I recognized my assassin. "Whistler. What was that?"

"Are you all right?" The question growled from him.

"I'm fine." What was wrong with him?

He remained tense and kept me pinned against the tree. "I saw you surrounded by guards and I couldn't reach you without causing a bloodbath. Then, they let you go."

"They did. They had no idea I was myself. Your disguise worked. I'm okay."

His grip on me still didn't soften. "I would have killed every single one of them if they'd tried to take you."

I had counted on it. "I know." I pushed my body into his and rested my hands on his shoulders, tilting my head up to see him properly.

His lips slammed onto mine, ravaging my mouth, pressing me harder into the trunk of the tree. I could taste his desperation, his fear, his need.

Mine bubbled up to match his.

I wrapped my arms around his neck, my legs around his waist as I opened to him. A violent sound rumbled through his chest as he reached up to grasp a handful of my hair. He yanked my head to the side and nipped down my throat, his facial hair scraping my tender flesh. He hadn't shaved that morning. Tendrils of pain morphed into pleasure as his pelvis ground into mine. The bark bit into my back, adding to the sensations.

He jerked back, his eyes wild. "You have to stop me. I can't. I'll hurt you."

His control was snapped. Thrills shot up my spine. Here was the real Whistler, stripped of masks.

I tried to pull him back. "You won't hurt me."

He remained stiff and distant. "You don't understand. I can't hold back."

"I don't want you to." Dammit, Whistler. If he didn't hurry, I'd change my mind.

He paused and pulled back a little more so he could see my face. "Do you know what I'm talking about?"

What I hoped was a seductive smile spread across my swollen lips. "Why don't you do your worst and find out?"

Wildfire burned through his eyes, banishing the usual calm and welcoming starlight. He yanked the bodice of my dress down with such force I heard a rip. Hated the dress anyway. My breasts spilled from the binding fabric and into his waiting hands.

His lips returned to mine while his fingers plucked and pinched my nipples, twisting them harshly. Another new experience for me and it almost shamed me how much I loved it. My pussy clenched with need and I cried out into his mouth, rubbing against him.

Whistler released my lips to bury his teeth in the crook of my neck. My fingers dug deeper into his shoulders as I burned, burned, burned. Every nip, every lick, every kiss, every touch sent fire scorching through me.

The sun trickled through the leaves, casting half of his face in shadows, the other half making his auburn hair flicker like flames, a demon sent to drag me off to hell.

I was more than willing to be dragged wherever he wished.

Unlike Saber, Whistler didn't whisper sweet nothings into my ear. He grunted and groaned and bit and pinched.

He yanked me away from the tree and my legs fell away from his waist. He spun me around and shoved me to the ground on my hands and knees, falling to his own knees behind me.

My hands flexed against the grass and soil as Whist flung the skirts of my dress up, cursing when he found the trousers beneath it. He pulled off first my boots, and then the pants until the cool air teased my ass.

His hands stroked my backside, warming me up. I pushed back against him, demanding more.

Whistler brought his palm sharply against my left cheek. "Patience."

I moaned and wiggled again, craving his harsh touch. He struck me again, fire spreading from my ass to my core. And again. And once more until I was positively soaked.

His fingers dipped into my wet folds, teasing my clit before he plunged them deep within me without warning. My cry echoed around us when he prodded and teased that special soft spot inside me. Another stroke, and then he was replacing his fingers with something much larger, something perhaps even larger than Saber's.

With a growl, Whist slammed all the way into me to the hilt, stretching me almost past my limits. I rode the edge of pleasure and pain as he fucked me hard and fast there in the dirt.

He spanked me again between thrusts, sharper smacks making me clench around him and push back against him. Our grunts and groans and the sounds of flesh slapping against each other were the only sounds in the surrounding woods. Even the birds were quiet, probably enjoying the show. He sank deep inside me, reaching a depth no one had ever plundered before.

Whist picked up his pace and reached around me to grab handfuls of my breasts, taking my nipples between his fingers and stretching them with such force, I felt it all the way to my pussy. My entire body flushed with roaring heat and a trembling began in my toes and swept through the rest of me. The fire flamed hotter and hotter until I swore I would combust and leave nothing but ashes behind.

My hands ripped up grass as the climax tore through me with a rippling violence. Whistler returned his grip to my hips, his fingers bruising in their strength.

He stiffened against me and a roar shook the limbs of the trees as he spilled himself inside me. Gentle hands stroked the warm and pulsing spots on my ass as we collected our breath.

Whistler slid out of me and helped me to my feet. "Are you all right?" Worry replaced the wildness in his eyes.

I smiled and reached up to cup his face in my palm. "I'm much better than all right."

"I didn't hurt you?" Why was he so worried?

"Whistler. You didn't do anything I didn't utterly enjoy."

He yanked me into him. "There's no way I can let you go. You were made for us. You're perfect. You're everything."

I kissed his neck and gave him a little nip. "You still haven't guessed my favorite dish."

With a snort, he released me. "I'm certain I figured it out. But you'll have to wait and see if I'm right. Now, come on. Let's try to get back so Sky and Saber don't come after us."

"You told them to wait until morning." I righted my clothes as best as I could, replacing the infernal dress with my shirt and cloak.

"I doubt they'll listen."

"This is trash. It was already trash, but you ripped it." I shoved the dress into my pack anyway. It could come in handy one day. Perhaps as dust rags.

Whist shined his smile on me again, bright and burning. "It's grown on me."

Indeed.

TWENTY-THREE

A bit sore and aching from Whist's rough treatment, we had to return more slowly on our way back to the safe house. I couldn't stop thinking about it the entire way back, remembering how hard and rough and filthy it was. How wild and free and uninhibited I felt. It was completely different from my time with Saber, but no more or less powerful and perfect. I couldn't help but wonder how it would be with Sky. He showed hints of dominance as well, at odds with his usual easygoing humor.

The three assassins were nothing like each other and I craved each one. I was starting to think I needed each one. Sky brought fun, laughter, companionship to my lonely life. Saber brought understanding and a shared love of music and art to my thirsty soul. And Whistler met my darkness with his own, turned my pain into something beautiful and strong.

What did I do for them? Something similar or different?

The safe house appeared at last and a warmth built around my heart. Almost like I'd just caught sight of home. Something I'd never had before. The assassins had brought me a lot of firsts.

My eyes were heavy with weariness, our trek took us deep into the night to make it back. The safe house sat in a pool of welcoming moonlight. Our steps sped up at the sight, glad to be back.

Inside, everything was dark, quiet. It made me nervous. Whist seemed to sense my unease because he smiled and held a finger to his lips and led me over to Sky and Saber's door. He cracked it open and leaned back for me to peer inside.

Moonlight streamed through the window, shining on the two naked men intertwined on the bed. I softened as I spied on them. Sky's arm was tossed carelessly over Saber's waist, half of Sky's ass peeking from beneath the covers.

I stepped back and Whist closed the door. I grinned at him over my shoulder as I opened my door, leaving it ajar for him to follow me inside.

He followed.

We stripped off our boots and outer clothes and climbed into the bed. He laid on his back and held an arm out for me to snuggle into his chest.

"You disappointed you weren't here to watch them?" I asked as I wiggled against him, trying to get comfortable.

"Not even a little."

"Do you ever join them?" The thought turned me on. All three of them, moving together in a beautiful dance of pleasure. Though I had a hard time imagining Whist indulging in his darker pleasures with them. They were both a little too alpha to enjoy it.

He rubbed his thumb against my upper arm. "Sometimes. But I prefer women and I don't have the same sort of bond with them that they have with each other. I'd rather watch them rather than take part."

"You sure seemed to enjoy taking part earlier." I grinned into his chest.

"It's different with you. And trust me, watching you with them is still almost as good as being inside you myself."

I squirmed against him, his words making me hot.

He kissed the top of my head. "Sleep, gorgeous. I'll fuck you again tomorrow."

How the hell was I supposed to sleep now?

TWENTY-FOUR

Sky and Saber woke us the following morning by bursting into the room and jumping into bed with us. Sky shoved Saber into it, right on top of me and Sky leapt onto Whist, smacking a kiss right on his lips.

Whist shoved him off with a curse, but Sky just squirmed until he snuggled between us. Saber rolled off me to my other side, spooning me from behind.

"At least you assholes have your clothes on." Whist grumbled the words, sleep still thickening his voice.

"We didn't want to show Rhapsody that side of us this soon." Sky poked my belly.

I swatted his hand away. "I've already seen your naked side."

"You haven't seen mine." Sky fake pouted.

I grinned at him. "I did last night."

Sky gasped dramatically. "Did someone spy on us while we were vulnerable and sleeping?"

"Maybe." I hid my face in his chest.

Sky scooted closer, trapping me between him and Saber. "You two should have climbed in with us. We were worried."

I shuddered, my nipples tightening. What would they do if I kissed Sky right now? Would the other two leave or would they join us?

"Clearly." Whist's dry voice pulled me away from my dirty musings.

Sky pushed his ass back to nudge Whist. "Oh shut up, Whist. You just wanted to have her for yourself a little longer."

Saber intervened before their bickering could continue. "How'd things go?"

Wiggling out from between the two assassins, I left Whist to recap our day together and disappeared into the bathroom. I still had dirt crusted in my nails and palms and probably my knees. Living with plumbing was the greatest luxury of my life. Returning to a life filled with bathing in streams was not appealing in the slightest.

I slipped into the tub brimming with steaming water and sighed. It still boggled my mind they went to such extremes for a mere safe house. Even my vivid imagination couldn't come up with a picture of what their actual home was like.

Too bad I'd never have a chance to find out for myself. I felt awful I'd stolen it away from them. Would they one day resent me for it?

But could I really take their choice away when I was so determined to make my own? When I spent all my time demanding the freedom to make choices for my life?

A tap on the door pulled me from my thoughts and I realized the bath had grown cold.

"You okay in there, doll? You're not hiding from us are you?"

"I'll be out in a minute, Sky." I unplugged the drain and stood, water sliding down my skin. I had a couple scrapes on my knees and my palms beneath the dirt from Whist's gentle ministrations. The sight made warmth trickle through me even though it stung. It was worth every second.

After toweling off, I slipping back into my then vacant room and got dressed. I'd been in the bath, lost in thought, for at least an hour.

I emerged, my wet hair still dripping down my back and found Whist holding out a plate with a treacle tart on it.

I stumbled back against the door. "Whistler. How the fuck? How did you guess?" I blinked hard, certain I was imagining things. There was no way.

"I'm just that good." His cocky smirk rivaled Sky's.

"Seriously? You cheated somehow." But I couldn't figure out how. "Tell me how you knew."

He stepped closer, the plate still held out to me. "It's going to take a lot for you to convince me to reveal my secrets."

I took the plate from him with trembling hands, my heart in my throat. "Guess you got your three weeks."

Whist's eyes softened, and he held out a chair for me at the table. Overwhelmed with crashing emotions, I used a fork to cut into the tart. Tears burned my eyes at the first bite. It tasted exactly like my mother's.

"You have a gift. I'm starting to suspect there's magic involved."

"You all right, love?" Saber rubbed my back.

"Yeah, I'm good. It's just been a really long time since I've had this." I paused, then decided to let them in. Just a little. "My mother used to make it for me when we had the money. It was always a rare treat, but we all loved it. She tried to teach me, but I'm an utter failure in the kitchen." Did Whist have any idea of the gift he gave me?

Based on the look in his eye, something fierce and protective and burning with complete understanding, made me think he had more than an inkling. How did he know me so well so soon? They all did.

And I thought I was beginning to know them as well. It terrified the fuck out of me.

Saber stroked my back once more, and we all turned our attention to dessert for breakfast. They gave me the space I needed to sort through my emotions. How did they do that? Know what I needed before I needed it?

For the first time, I wished my parents were kindreds. Then, maybe I wouldn't have been so confused, uncertain which was the magic of them and which was the magic of the bond.

"What's the plan now?" Sky asked. "The guards are still searching for our girl here. It won't be long before they make their way out here once she doesn't show up in villages."

"All the surrounding villages have more guards than usual." Whist passed around mugs of coffee.

I almost choked on my bite of the tart. "Wait. When did you find that out? You didn't mention it to me."

"I overheard a couple villagers whispering about it when the guards came into the tavern. Word has gotten around. I'm surprised the owner let you play. It's going to be hard on all bards for a while. They let you go once you convinced them you were someone else, but it's making people uneasy."

My ears perked up at his choice of words.

Whist read the hope on my face and shook his head. "Not uprising kind of uneasy. Wary of musicians kind of uneasy. Most people don't want change, gorgeous. Failgrey is a prosperous country. More people find their kindreds than not and everyone pretends the single ones or the ones whose kindreds are fucked up don't exist."

Before I could start ranting and railing against the system, someone kicked in the door.

TWENTY-FIVE

The assassins leapt to their feet, chairs falling to the floor behind them.

Whist whipped a fork at the face of the royal guard in the doorway. "Sky. Get Rhapsody out of here. You know where to meet. We're blown."

Sky picked me up out of my chair while Whist and Saber unearthed weapons out of thin air. Where the fuck were they hiding all those? Sky hustled me towards the back door.

I struggled against his grip. "Wait. My pack. My ukulele."

Sky didn't stop. "There's no time. We have to move."

A sob caught in my throat, panic clawing at me. I couldn't lose Papa's ukulele. It would shatter me. "It's the only thing I have left, Sky. Please."

"I'm so sorry, doll. We'll try to come back for it. I swear. But there are more than just that one lug and Saber and Whist will be distracted if they have to worry about you. Please, Rhapsody."

Another sob tore from my throat, but I let Sky drag me away, no longer fighting, but not helping either. Outside, four guards waited for us. And based on the crashing noises inside, more had joined Saber and Whist.

We were trapped.

Sky shoved me behind him and the air rang with the scrape of steel as he drew his sword. "You're a burr on my ass, got it?"

I sniffed and nodded. "Yeah."

He squeezed my arm and then he was moving, spinning, slicing, cutting, killing. It was like a dance. I could almost hear the music. Shock kept me frozen and I could do nothing but watch.

A song came together in my mind—this one crying out my grief and burgeoning love for my assassins. One about the agony of choices, but the freedom in having them. The lyrics were still a jumble, but the music was crystal clear.

Could Sky hear it? He moved perfectly to the beat in my head. Perhaps I was adjusting the beat to him. There was such a strange beauty in his killing, stark and harsh. His body swelled in protection. His movements calm and certain. His eyes burning with a sort of holy vengeance.

If I could paint, I would have painted him. Just like this.

I hated waiting on the sidelines, unable to help for fear of getting in the way. Two lessons did not turn me into a fighter. I'd always fought with my words, with my music. Only occasionally had I used my dagger and only as a last resort.

Maybe it was time for me to take up a sword.

Sky stumbled and the remaining guard raised his sword to strike. Before my brain caught up, I belted out a song as loud as I could. The guard jerked with surprise and his eyes darted over to me. It gave Sky the opening he needed to smash the hilt of his sword into the guard's face and knock him unconscious to the ground.

Sky's wide eyes met mine. "You just saved my life. With song."

I stuttered a little before I could push words out of my stiff lips. "I guess I did."

He wrapped me in his arms, breathing in the scent of my hair. "That's definitely a first for me."

"Hopefully a last."

He set me back on the ground and pulled me away from the house. "Keep it in your arsenal just in case. I'm willing to wager it would work again."

I dug in my heels. "Wait. What about Saber and Whist?"

He tugged on my arm. "I have my orders and they're to get you out of here."

"But they might need help." I cast a desperate, fearful glance over my shoulder, hoping for a glimpse of the others.

"Trust me. They'll be fine. More guards will be on the way. We have to go."

Before I could argue further, the other two assassins tumbled through the door, Whist holding up a bleeding Saber who held my ukulele in his arms.

I rushed over to them, ignoring the instrument, and reached out, my hand hovering over the slice on Saber's arm. "What happened?"

"He went after your ukulele and got a sword to the arm for his trouble." Whist shook his head.

My mouth dropped in horror as I relieved him of my most precious possession. "Saber, I'm so sorry. I didn't mean for you to put yourself in danger for that."

Saber's uninjured arm reached out to run his hand along my shoulder. "It was your father's. You need it."

"I need you more." The words escaped my mouth before I could stop them. But I meant every one.

Whist nudged us towards the woods. "We need to get out of here. More will be coming and the closest safe house is half a day away."

"Why don't we steal the guards' horses? They might make the trip faster." I wasn't a confident rider, but I knew how. And I wanted them far away from danger.

Sky grinned. "You'd make a decent assassin, doll. Just wait until you two hear how Rhapsody here saved my life."

I rolled my eyes and remained close to Saber's side. "He needs to be stitched up."

"I'm fine, love. Once we get away from here, we'll stop and you can tend to me, all right?" Saber patted my hand.

"Fine." Avoiding his wound, I raised up and pressed a kiss to his cheek. "And thank you."

"Anytime, love."

I scowled and shook my head so hard my braid whipped me in the face. "No. Not again. Nothing is more precious than your life."

"It was worth it just to see you smile."

"I think the blood loss is making you cheesy. You're usually smoother than that." I ignored how even cheesy, his words made me melt.

He smiled. "I'll do better next time."

Whist broke up the moment by leading over two horses. "Rhapsody, you're with me. Sky, you take Saber."

"Splitting up or staying together?" Sky asked.

"Split up. Circular route and meet in the middle." Whist's words made no sense to me, but Sky seemed to understand them.

"See you in about an hour."

"We'll probably beat you there so we'll wait." Whist tossed me into the saddle and leapt up behind me, his hands coming around to grasp the reins.

I still clutched the ukulele to my chest, some of Saber's blood splattered across it. My heart clenched at what could have happened just because Saber wanted to make me happy. Why did he do that for someone he'd only known a few days, kindred or not?

I didn't understand.

TWENTY-SIX

We galloped for twenty minutes with only the whipping wind as company.

I needed to take my mind off my worries for Saber. "Can you explain the kindred bond a little better for me?"

"What do you mean?" Whist asked.

"My parents weren't kindred, and we were never close to anyone, so I was never told much about it from people who have personal experience." It was still a mystery even though I was surrounded by it and it was an integral part of our world.

I didn't like mysteries.

"All right. What specifically do you want to know about it?"

Questions flew from my mouth almost faster than my lips could form them. "How strong is it? Does it override free will? Does it make you do things you wouldn't normally do? I know it's possible to not accept the bond, but that it's extremely painful."

"Kindred bonds are incredibly strong, but it doesn't take away your choices. You can choose to accept it or choose not to. Few people go against it and not just because of the pain, but because of how their kindred fits them so perfectly. When we found you, it was like a piece I didn't even realize I was missing clicked inside me and made me whole. Being with you hasn't changed my personality or made me do things any differently than I usually would.

But I feel complete now. Mainly, all the kindred bond does is draw the best matches to each other. It helps you recognize each other. Whether that's just two people of it's five. There are tons of books and songs and poems and studies written about it, but it remains our biggest mystery."

"Thanks. That helps." Sort of.

"Believe me. Saber putting himself in harms way to do something for someone he cares about is completely normal for him. He's always doing thoughtful shit like that." How did Whist read me so well? It was frustrating the hell out of me. I wasn't used to being seen or understood.

"Unlike you."

He ignored my dry tone. "Exactly."

"Says the big, bad assassin who somehow took the time to figure out my favorite food and make it for me. Are you saying the bond didn't make you do that?"

"It did, but not in the way you're implying. With you, I'm finally able to be my true self and allow some of my vulnerabilities to show. Maybe it's the bond, maybe it's just you. I'm actually leaning towards thinking it's just you. Not all bonds settle this quickly. Usually there's a longer period of awkwardness and getting to know each other. But like I have been saying. You fit right in with us, almost seamlessly." A kiss tickled the back of my neck and I sank back against him.

He clucked at the horse, urging him along faster. My mind refused to stop whirling with information, my chest heavy with fear. I was losing myself in them. And they were giving everything up for me, even willing to give their lives.

It was all way too much.

Somehow, I fell asleep on the back of the horse. Whist nudged me awake when Sky and Saber arrived. I scrambled from the back of the horse, worried eyes roving over Saber.

"I'm fine. Sky wrapped me up while we rode. He's surprisingly good at steering a horse with only his thighs." Saber smiled over at Sky who winked back.

I hesitated. "Maybe I should look at it just in case."

Sky shot me a reassuring smile. "I'm always the medic of our group, doll. I've gotten really good at patching them up over the years."

"Fine." I wasn't very reassured, but I didn't want to hurt him more by poking at it.

"We'll take a quick break here and then back on the move."

"How the fuck did they find us?" The anger in Sky's voice shocked me. He'd shown flashes of seriousness, but the anger was new. It was kind of hot.

Whist looked grim. "The other assassins must have given us up."

Sky drew back a step, shaking his head. "They wouldn't."

Apparently, they were close with the other assassins. More people they were leaving behind.

Whist rubbed at our horse's neck. "They would if the king demanded it. That's the only location we've ever shared, so we'll be safe at the other one for now."

"I don't understand. I haven't started a revolution. Why does the king want me dead so badly?" It still didn't make sense. I was nobody.

Whist winced. "He didn't before. But now you've corrupted three of his assassins. He is probably now fearing a revolution. If he knew you were our kindred, he'd probably still want you dead, but it would definitely calm him down."

Perhaps they'd even get their lives back. If they told the king they were protecting their kindred, he'd understand. He'd have to. It was his laws that made kindreds so important.

The seed of an idea planted itself in my mind even while my soul screamed out at me against it. But the assassins weren't the only ones who would do whatever it took to keep the ones they cared about safe and happy.

"It's my turn with Rhapsody." Sky grabbed me around the waist and spun me in a circle before lifting me into the saddle. I grinned dizzily down at him.

I would soak up every minute I had left with my three assassins. The end loomed dark and near. I just hoped I had the courage to do what was right. If I could only figure out what that was.

We rode another three hours before we turned off the trail and crashed through thick trees and bushes. Sky protected me from the branches whipping towards my face. We finally broke into a clearing and there sat a house with a small orchard stretching out behind it.

Whist helped Saber off the horse while Sky assisted me. My jaw dropped when I stepped inside.

The second safe house was even more elaborate than the first. "This is just ridiculous. Shouldn't places like this be rustic shacks? How do you keep them up?"

Saber leaned against the wall with a sigh. "We travel a lot for work so one of us is always available to do a little upkeep. A couple of them are like what you imagine, but we don't use them as often."

"How well do assassinations pay?" I asked.

"Very well. The king believes fear and money keep people loyal to him," Saber said.

"Well, the king has proved many times that he's a moron. Too bad he didn't take after his grandmother." The king's father had been the one to make non-kindred marriage illegal. And the current king had done nothing to change that.

"No arguments here, gorgeous." Whist scowled through the back window at his garden. "I'll be cleaning out the beds for days."

"Worry about it tomorrow. We're almost out of light and we are all exhausted." Sky turned to me with a mischievous grin. "There's something we want to show you."

They led me to the very back of the house to a room at the end of the hall. Inside was a gorgeous bedroom decorated in beautiful shades of green. And in the center of the room sat the most ridiculously massive bed I'd ever seen in my life. It would've easily fit seven or eight hulking men.

"I take it we're sharing tonight?" The corner of my lips rose.

Sky grinned. "Yes, but just sleep. Saber needs to heal and it would be mean to play if he can't join."

"I don't mind watching like Whist this time." Saber shut the door behind us.

I still hadn't made my mind up of what to do. I couldn't bear for them to touch me that way before I made my decision. "We're all exhausted anyway. Napping on horses is not restful."

Whist searched my eyes like he suspected the direction my thoughts were headed, but he asked no questions. The four of us kicked off boots and shucked off cloaks and collapsed onto the giant mattress.

A symphony of groans rose through the air as we nestled together on our bed of clouds.

TWENTY-SEVEN

I resisted the comfort of the bed and being wrapped up between Whist and Sky and laid awake long into the night. My brain refused to shut up and grant me any peace.

As we rode, I had finally realized where we were. And coincidentally enough, their safe house wasn't far from mine. It would take me half a day on foot to reach it.

My little shack still had a decent collection of tinned food and I still had a few coins in the hidden pocket of my cloak. It was enough to get me through the winter months. I could remain hidden until spring and perhaps by then the king would be onto the next person who irritated him. If the assassins returned to the king and explained I was their kindred, but had disappeared, they'd be forgiven. The king couldn't expect them to kill me, it was impossible anyway. They could return to their families, friends, lives.

They wouldn't be in danger anymore.

If they stayed with me, they would always be at risk. They would always put their lives on the line to keep me safe. I couldn't give up my music. It would break something inside of me to stop playing my songs. And somehow, they understood it and supported it.

But they deserved more than a life on the run, hopping from one place to another. I was used to it. It was my whole life, and it was miserable.

I wouldn't condemn them to the same fate. I cared about them too much. It wasn't yet love, but it was headed there. It would be better for all of us if we ended it now before we learned to love each other.

At least the three of them would still be together.

I slid out from between them and Whist cracked open an eye. "You all right, gorgeous?"

Heat in my throat, I kissed him lightly. "Yeah. Go back to sleep. I have to use the washroom."

He grunted and rolled over closer to Sky. My chest tightened at the sight, but I memorized it. This was how I wanted to remember them. The three of them crowded together, limbs tangled, different shades of naked skin gleaming in the moonlight.

I grabbed my boots and cloak from the floor and slipped out to the main room. I waited twenty minutes to be sure they were asleep and weren't coming to look for me, then grabbed my ukulele and left.

Tears poured down my cheeks and a yawning cavern split my heart in two as I stumbled away into the dark night. I kept my eyes lowered, too scared to look up at the stars and remind myself of Whistler's eyes. My choice was made, I couldn't afford to weaken now.

My body trembled and shook like I was coming down from an opium addiction. The kindred bond may not have been completed, but it was damn close. And leaving them was killing me.

Over time, it wouldn't be so bad. I hoped.

I hurried my steps, worried they were experiencing the same pain and would be after me before the morning woke them. If I'd taken one of the horses, it would have gotten me away farther faster, but I couldn't take anything else from them.

They'd need the horses to return to the palace.

The pain sharpened, and I stumbled to my knees with a cry. I hadn't expected it to be this bad. It wasn't the last time I ran from them.

But the last time, I hadn't slept with any of them. The last time, I hadn't gotten to know them. I still fought against the bond. I wasn't fighting it anymore.

Had I accepted the bond? Was the pain telling me I was too late?

There was usually a ceremony to accept it, but maybe it was a tradition built only for show. I hated how little I knew and understood about it.

I dragged myself back to my feet and forced myself to keep moving, needing at least another hour between me and their house before I could stop. Hopefully, they wouldn't figure out which direction I went in.

Just a little farther and I'd stop to rest.

I wasn't sure how long I wandered, barely aware of where I was or where I was going. Grief and pain ravaged me, making it difficult to focus. I was ashamed of myself, never expecting to be this pathetic over a man. Or three.

I was stronger than this. My whole adult life and most of my later childhood years were spent alone. I was used to it. A few days with a few handsome men wouldn't change that.

It had been an exhausting week, I was stumbling tired. I had to stop. Just for a moment. I'd catch my breath and then be on my way again.

The darkness of the night lightened to gray. Clouds coated the sky, hiding the sun, warning of rain. It matched my mood, how appropriate.

The pain wasn't as sharp. I was getting used to it and the bond was loosening. It made the tears fall harder, tears I hadn't been able to stop since I walked out the door. I'd given up trying. I missed the pain. At least with it, I still felt connected to them. But the farther I walked, the more it faded.

The only pain in me now was the grief of losing them.

Fog rolled through the trees, making it harder for me to see where I was headed. I should have stopped, but I continued on since I wasn't hurting as badly.

I wiped my face on my cloak, determined to pull myself together. I was being ridiculous. I made the right choice. It was best for them and it was possibly even best for me.

A figure appeared through the fog, and I was certain I was hallucinating until it tackled me to the ground.

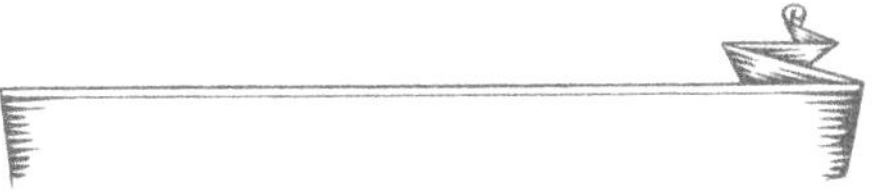

TWENTY-EIGHT

"Whistler." His name sighed from my lips as the last bit of pain disappeared. The bond wasn't weakening, he had just been getting closer.

He pinned me to the ground and loomed over me. "What the fuck do you think you're doing?" He snarled the question in my face.

"I was doing what was best for the three of you. You can go back to your lives without me. You won't be in danger." I tried to shove him off me, but he refused to budge.

His hands tightened on my shoulders. "We're fucking assassins, Rhapsody. We're always in danger."

I winced at his use of my given name. I loved their pet names for me, how they each had their own. "You have family and friends back at the palace."

"But we don't have you." He all but roared his fury, and it echoed around us.

The fog surrounding us made him seem almost otherworldly, his red hair the only color I could see.

I closed my eyes against his fury and against my agony. "One day, you'd resent me for all you'd have to give up to be with me."

He shook me, my back bumping against the ground. "The only fucking thing we'd resent you for is leaving us. You know, you go on and on about choices and freedom and then you go and rip ours away from us. We chose you, you maddening woman. And you threw it back in our faces. You didn't even leave a note. You just disappeared with guards and assassins crawling all over the country searching for you."

Tears reemerged and slid down my face. He was right. I was acting like only my choices mattered. My choice to continue singing. My choice to leave them. My choice to deny the bond. My choice to remain in this country.

And every single choice was wrong.

"I'm sorry." My voice broke as I tried to swallow the tears and gather my wits.

Whist crushed his body into mine. "Oh, trust me. You will be. You will be very sorry when I'm finished with you."

I quivered at the dark promise.

His eyes flashed, and I felt him harden against me, but he shook his head. "Not here. Sky and Saber are out searching for you in the other direction so they'll meet us back at the house."

He leapt to his feet and dragged me along with him. As angry as he was, his grip on me was gentle. Sniffling, I followed him through the foggy morning over to the horse.

It mystified me how I had missed the sound of him riding up.

Whist helped me onto the back of the animal and threw himself up behind me. He kept a stony silence as we rode back to the house. I didn't try to break it, too mired in confused thoughts and feelings.

Mist soaked through my clothes, plastering it to my body. When I shuddered, Whist held me closer to share his warmth.

Finally, I spoke, unable to bear it anymore. "I really am sorry. I regretted it the moment I walked out the door, but I thought I was doing what was right."

Whist clucked to the horse, urging her on faster. "I understand, gorgeous. I really do. But we had a deal. Three weeks. It hasn't even been one. I'm not saying you have to accept us, but at least do us the courtesy of telling us and saying goodbye."

My eyes slid closed in misery. "I knew I wouldn't be able to leave if I told the three of you. I wouldn't have the strength to let you go."

"We don't ever want you to let us go unless it's something you want for yourself." His words were so perfect, it was still difficult to believe he and the others were real.

They said everything I ever wanted and a lot I hadn't realized I needed. They didn't trap me, they offered me freedom. I kept waiting for the catch.

"I never expected to have this. I thought I'd always be alone and then the three of you crashed into my life and it changed everything I thought I knew and believed."

He sighed, the force of it rattling his chest. "I know. Just take it day by day. We've accepted the bond. We want you. We chose you. It's completely up to you what we do next. Just don't run from us again."

The fog was lifting, from the air and from my head. I could see deeper through the forest and I my future was less murky as well.

"I think I did accept it. It felt like it was killing me every step I took away from you three."

"It felt like that for us too." He clutched me even tighter, like he was afraid I would disappear from his arms.

"I'm sorry, Whistler." I was. Devastatingly so.

A growl thundered in his chest. "I love it when you say my whole name. No one else does. Not even my mother."

"I like your full name. But I don't like it when you use mine. It makes me feel like I'm in trouble."

He released the reins with one of his hands and slid it up my thigh, stopping before he reached where I wanted him most. "Oh, gorgeous. You have no idea the trouble coming for you. I meant what I said. You will be begging me for mercy when I'm done with you."

My nipples hardened and sent a bolt straight to my core. "I'm looking forward to it."

"And when I'm through with you, you'll have Sky and Saber to answer to."

I wasn't looking forward to that quite as much. I didn't want to see Sky's laughing eyes dulled with pain and betrayal. I didn't want to lose Saber's sweetness to disappointment and sorrow.

"Are they mad at me too?" I asked in a small voice.

"Very. And hurt. And worried." He returned his hand to the reins as we took a fork in the road.

I harrumphed. "You couldn't lie to me? Or sugarcoat it?" I was super nervous about seeing Sky and Saber. Whist was shitty enough, but fighting with him didn't pain me as much as it did the others. Whist brought out my combative side and a part of me enjoyed it. He understood the angry, bitter part of me because he was the same. The others didn't have such darkness. Or if they did, I had yet to uncover it.

"Sorry. Not my style." He released the reins again and his hand slid under my shirt to rest on the bare skin of my stomach.

I tucked my head into the crook of his neck, hoping his hand would travel higher. "I know."

Whist took the hint, and he slid his hand up me ribs, grazing the undersides of my breasts. I squirmed on the back of the horse, craving friction, but it wasn't enough.

It was nowhere near enough.

By the time the house came back into sight, the sun had completely appeared over the horizon and I trembled with desire and a slight hint of trepidation.

Whist had kept up teasing touches and steady innuendos for the remainder of the ride until I was ready to beg him to take me in the forest again like the last time. But I wanted to play the game the way he wanted. I wanted to see what he had in store for me. And the mist would have made things quite muddy and uncomfortable.

The other horse was still missing, so Sky and Saber weren't there. "Should we go look for them?" I asked once Whist settled the horse in the small paddock.

Whist shook his head and stood aside for me to enter the house. "No. We have two hours until they return. We would ride five hours in each direction and then come back to report. Where were you headed anyway?"

I nibbled on my bottom lip before I answered. "There's a house. One I lived in with my parents at the end. It's in the middle of nowhere and no one knows about it."

"Still had some secrets, eh?" He raised a brow.

"Not anymore." I spun around to face him.

"Good." The door slammed shut behind us. "Strip. Now."

TWENTY-NINE

I took a steadying breath and with fumbling hands and fingers; I removed my clothes. There was no grace or seduction to my movements. I was too nervous and excited and ready.

Whist stared at me once I was naked before him. "If you tell me to stop, I will. If I hurt you, tell me. Understand?"

"Yes. Please, Whistler. I can't wait anymore." I needed him. Desperately.

His eyes darkened and then he was on me, savage and wild. Before I realized what was happening, I was slammed against the wall and his mouth covered mine, drinking each whimper and moan, one of his hands wrapped around my throat.

I tried to reach for him, but he captured my wrists with one of his hands and stretched them over my head, trapping them against the wall. I was caught and had no desire to be freed. His other hand explored my body—plucking my nipples, grabbing my ass, teasing my pussy.

He sank his teeth into my skin at the juncture of my neck and shoulder and I thrashed, desperate to touch him, to get him inside me.

"Please. Please. Please." I chanted the words.

He licked the bite mark to soothe the sting. "Please what?"

"Fuck me. Punish me. Something. I need you, Whistler." I struggled against his grip on my wrists.

A growl rumbled in his chest, vibrating through me. He jerked me away from the wall and shoved me face down over the sofa. I scrambled to keep from smothering in the cushions and steadied myself with my arms grasping the back of the sofa.

I heard his belt and trousers hit the floor, and I trembled in anticipation, lifting onto my toes.

His hand whipped onto my ass, with much greater force than before. I yelped in surprise, but the moment of pain burned and morphed into want. He slid his hand between my legs and pinched my slippery clit. It shot fire through me. His touch always burned and I craved getting closer and closer to the flames until they consumed me.

I spread my legs wider, wanting more, wanting it harder, wanting it to hurt. He slipped his fingers up my crack and circled my back hole. My breath caught. I was still a virgin there, but I'd always wanted to try it, I'd just never trusted anyone enough.

I trusted my assassins though.

Instead of pushing into it, Whist spanked me again. I moaned and pushed my ass back towards him.

"Prepare yourself," he growled.

For what?

He nudged my legs apart a little farther, opening me up. Then he really began to spank me. He brought his hand down on a different part of my ass with each strike. Not a single inch of my ass or the tops of my thighs were left untouched. Again and again and again. A couple times it struck directly on my pussy or asshole, making my stomach jolt.

My ass burned and I could feel my heartbeat pulse in my ass. He paused and dipped back into my core, feeling how soaked I was for him. He stroked a finger along the left cheek and I pushed back again, wanting more. He stroked my ass again, like he was giving me the chance to stop him. But I never wanted to stop.

I never thought I would love pain mixed with my pleasure.

"Your ass turns such a lovely shade of red, gorgeous. I want to paint you with this color every fucking night."

I moaned. "You'll get no arguments from me."

He spanked me once more, and I almost came.

And then he was inside me, finally fucking me, and I was coming, hard. But he didn't stop. He kept going, harder and harder, inside me so deep I thought he might rip me in half.

Every time he sank into me, he rubbed against the burning flesh of my ass. He nipped and sucked and kissed along my back, his guttural groans gasping in my ear.

"Harder, please, Whistler."

He gripped my hips and slammed so hard I saw stars. And I came completely undone. I screamed out and fell apart, the climax so strong, I almost passed out.

Whistler slammed into me again and yanked my upper body up against his, cupping my jaw. His cock twitched inside me as he came. My knees buckled, and he caught me, keeping me from falling to the floor in a heap.

With now gentle hands, he settled me on the cushions and wrapped me in a blanket. With his hand anchored on the back, he leapt over the sofa and sat next to me, pulling me into him.

"Are you all right?" He sounded concerned.

I wrapped my arm around his middle. "Very." And I was. But I loved how he kept checking in on me, how he wanted me to enjoy his touch, harsh as it was.

His fingers dug into my back, soothing the sore muscles until I was boneless against him. My backside was sore, but in a pleasant way.

"Damn, gorgeous. You are something special." He repositioned me until I was reclined across from him, and drew one of my legs into his lap, massaging my calves and moving his way up my thighs.

I groaned and stretched. "You're not too bad yourself."

"Is this sort of thing new for you?" He took my other leg and gave it the same attention as the other.

I chuckled lightly. "Yes. Most of my other encounters were mere tumbles in the back rooms of inns. Nothing special or all that satisfying."

"That's a damn shame. You were meant to be worshiped. Cherished. Pleasured." With each word, he pressed a kiss to my leg.

My legs fell open, wordlessly begging for more. Always more, more, more.

He smiled and adjusted us on the sofa, my blanket falling away, until I was on my back with one of my legs dangling to the floor and the other thrown over the back of the sofa. Whist knelt between my spread thighs. He shot me a wicked grin and bent his head towards my center. He licked lightly with teasing strokes. My back arched, and I dug my palms into my forehead. His tender touch after such rough love-making made my head spin.

He kept me riding the edge, never pushing me over. I was soaked and desperate and breathless. I hated it and I loved it. I wanted to ride this feeling forever, and I wanted to curse him until he granted me release.

The front door slammed open and Saber and Sky spilled inside, their eyes wild. "Is she here? Did you find her?"

THIRTY

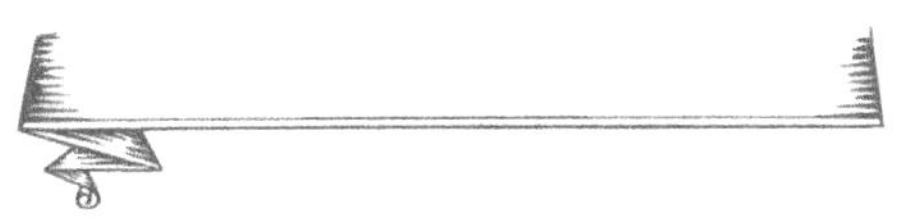

Their mouths fell open at the sight of Whistler and I naked with his head buried between my legs.

Sky stripped off his clothes. "I see you got her warmed up for us, Whist."

Whistler sat back, and I whimpered in protest. "Don't worry, gorgeous. The night is nowhere near over."

Saber closed the door and his clothes dropped to the floor beside Sky's. "Isn't she delicious?"

Whistler bent over and sucked on my clit once before raising back up. "Even better than my cooking."

Too far gone to properly appreciate the ridiculousness of that statement, I whimpered again when Whist climbed from between my legs.

Sky plucked me into his arms over the back of the sofa. "We need more room than that tiny thing." He carried me differently from Saber. Sky tossed me over his shoulder, holding me by the back of my thighs, giving me a great view of his ass.

He kicked open the door of the room we slept in last night. A shard of pain shot through me at the sight of the remains of their panic when they woke to find me gone. The bed was ravaged, most of the blankets tangled and on the floor. A lantern was broken on the floor in the corner. Like someone had thrown it against the wall.

Sky tossed me onto the bed and I bounced against the mattress, my eyes wide as I took in the sight of the three of them standing there naked, their cocks hard and huge. Standing together like that, I could see the differences in size and shape, but they were all more well-endowed than any man I'd been with before.

Sky and Saber joined me, climbing on either side of me. Whistler remained in the corner of the room, apart, but watching, giving the others their turn.

Two different hands stroked and explored me. One was sensual, the other playful. I reached out to return the favor, my fingers brushing against the muscles on their chests and stomachs.

Nerves skittered up and down my spine at the thought of both of them taking me together. How was it even going to work?

Saber pulled Sky to him across my body and they kissed, tongues tangling, Saber's hand buried in Sky's dark curls, their cocks digging into my sides.

Heat pooled in my belly and electricity hummed through my veins. Fuck, they were beautiful.

Sky reached over me and took Saber into his hand, pumping up and down on Saber's cock. My fingers explored Sky's, my thumb brushing his tip. They both shuddered and broke the kiss, returning their attention to me.

Saber covered my mouth with his, his tongue tracing my lips, asking them to open for him.

Sky bent over my chest, taking one of my nipples in his mouth. He flicked his tongue over it and sucked it deep into his mouth. I writhed and moaned into Saber's mouth, trying to stay mindful of his wound.

Sky bit my nipple and I almost shot off the bed, completely overcome. It was too much. Too much pleasure, too many sensations.

It was too much and not enough.

"Please." My plea rasped from my throat.

"We've got you, love." Saber soothed me, cupping my face and kissing me with heartbreaking softness. He put everything he felt into his kiss, speaking without words of his devotion and worry and need.

I stretched my neck up to speak his same language. My kiss expressed my regret, my acceptance, my burgeoning love.

Sky grabbed my hands and hauled me up to a seated position while Saber scooted up against the headboard and rested his back against it.

"Get on your hands and knees, doll." Sky's voice whipped through the room with command.

I shivered and scrambled to obey, facing Saber, with Sky behind me.

"Since Saber is still recovering, we're going to take it easy on him tonight. But he'll be feeling better soon enough and then you'll have all three of us fucking you ragged." Sky slid his hand from the nape of my neck, down to my ass, teasing my back hole. "We're going to take you there. Soon. You'll have three cocks inside you at once."

I mewled and shifted. "Please." It was the only word I still remembered how to say. I was lost. Lost in them, in their touch, their scents, their words.

He rubbed my still sore ass and loosed a wicked chuckle. "I see Whist gave you a spanking you so richly deserved. Your ass is still red. Pity I wasn't here to help."

If someone didn't touch me, fuck me, spank me, or something, I would scream.

Or take care of the aching need pulsing through my veins myself.

"Crawl over to Saber. Touch him."

My arms trembled as I scrabbled across the huge bed and between Saber's legs. I ran my hands up his hard, smooth thighs, brushing his skin with kisses and licks.

One of Saber's hands tangled in my hair and he caressed my head. I took his cock into my hand, marveling at the steel wrapped in silky softness. I wrapped my fingers around his thick girth and pumped up and down. His hips lifted from the bed and his eyes slid shut.

Sky rewarded me with his fingers between my legs, rubbing at my clit. I flicked a glance over to the corner where Whist still stood, slowly stroking himself, his eyes burning into me.

"Have you ever taken a man into your mouth, doll?" Sky circled my clit before he sank three fingers inside, then pulled back out.

"Once or twice." It was something I enjoyed, making a man come undone at my touch, completely under my power.

"Show me." Sky's hand pressed on my back.

I held Saber by the base of his cock and took him into my mouth. He tasted just like he smelled, smooth and smoky. His moan harmonized with mine and I played him like he was an instrument.

Sky plunged inside me and I groaned around Saber. It took a few moments, but then we were moving completely in sync, a dance of pleasure. I could see Whist from the corner of my eye matching his movements with ours.

I took Saber deeper, relaxing my throat and swallowing around him. He hissed and his hand jerked in my hair.

Two cocks pinned me between them. I couldn't imagine adding Whistler into the mix, but I was desperate to find out.

Sky pulled out of me and I mewled in dismay. He shushed me and dipped two fingers inside before slamming back into me. His wet fingers returned to my ass, and he pushed one into the tight ring.

Warmth started in my center and spread out throughout the rest of my body. Sky added a second finger to my ass, stretching me. He moved slowly at first, getting me used to it, and then he was slamming his hand against me in time with his dick.

I was filled and overflowing with pleasure and passion, the blood in my veins rushing to my head, roaring in my ears.

At the first taste of Saber's pleasure, I joined him in climax, barely able to swallow as cries of bliss crawled up my throat.

Like a game of dominoes, Sky and Whist followed us.

Sky and I collapsed onto Saber as Whist stumbled over to the bed and fell beside us, joining our pile.

THIRTY-ONE

We curled up there for almost an hour recovering, snuggled together in the center of the bed. Sky was the one to finally break the peace between us.

He scooted away from me, dropping the corner of a blanket over his lap. "Ready to explain yourself, doll?"

I drew my knees up to my chest. "I'm sorry. I thought I was doing what was best for the three of you."

Sky raised a brow. "I take it Whist helped you see the folly of that sort of thought?"

I bit my bottom lip and shot a glance at Whist's expressionless face. "He did. Although I still think you'd all be better off. I'm worried one day you'll regret it."

In a rare flash of frustration, Saber yanked my feet and slid me down the bed until I laid flat beneath him, naked and vulnerable and sorry. "We will never regret finding you and choosing you. You are the answer to every secret hope of our hearts. We couldn't have picked a kindred better if we'd wished for you. Other than your infernal stubborn hardheadedness. I could certainly do without that. And if you run from us again without a word, Whist won't be the only one turning that beautiful ass of yours red. And I won't use a hand." His eyes flashed as he took in my hardened nipples.

Sky flicked one of the rosy buds, making me jerk. "Saber has a dark side as well, doll. It just takes a lot more to bring it out of him. I'm afraid you've tied yourself to a trio of assholes."

"Luckily I've got more than a little asshole in me too." I cupped Saber's face in my hand, rubbing my thumb across his cheekbone, watching him soften. He kissed the top of my breast, my hand sliding around to the back of his head as he laid down on me, using my chest as a pillow.

Even after hours fucking, I still wanted them. Still ached for them.

Whist snorted from the other side of Sky. "You might be worse than us."

I shoved away the lingering tendrils of lust. I may have wanted more, but my body needed to recover. "I tried to tell you I am way more trouble than I'm worth."

Saber rolled off me and scowled. "And we told you, we don't fucking care. You're ours. You're worth everything."

I gulped and sat up, looking each one in the face. It was time. There was no way I could leave them, we were tied together for better or for worse. And I needed to tell them that. To banish the lingering hurt and doubts in their eyes.

"I was wrong. I never should have left you three. But I don't need the three weeks to make my decision."

Flashes of worry flickered across their faces.

I tangled my hands together in my lap to keep them still. "I've decided to accept the bond. I want to be with the three of you. If that means moving to another country, to Havisam, I'll do it. Whatever it takes for us to make a life together." It wasn't fair to ask them to bend over backwards for me. My parents understood love even if they weren't kindreds. They sacrificed everything, eventually even their lives, for love. They wouldn't begrudge me the same.

Silence fell for a moment and I shifted nervously. Had they changed their minds?

They leapt onto me at the same time, burying me beneath a pile of happy, naked assassins.

I grinned and returned their kisses and embraces and watched as they kissed and embraced each other. After so many years alone, I finally had a family again.

I was home.

Thank you for reading, and I hoped you enjoyed meeting Rhapsody and her handsome fellows. If you did, I would really appreciate it if you left an honest review on Amazon. It helps so much.

Next up, Rhapsody and her assassins will be headed on their most dangerous adventure yet. The second book will be out soon.

I also write Urban Fantasy and Fairy Tale retellings as Harley Gordon. Feel free to check them out while you wait for the next book in Kindred Souls.

Bo Peep spent years as a Librarian for the Faery Tale Administration, but after her human family died, she blamed Faery for her loss and disappeared.

Until the Mad Hatter shows up with news of her most hated enemy.

Bo must strap her sword back on and reenter the world she swore she was through with, alongside the only man who makes her blood boil.

One last job before she gets sucked back into their stories and forgets that happily ever after is usually a lie.

ABOUT THE AUTHOR

An expert in parkour, Helene Gadot moonlights as a Nail Polish Namer and occasional ghostwriter. She lives with her husband and trio of rugrats in the South. Helene has a serious coffee mug and throw pillow addiction, and when she isn't reading or writing, she's probably shopping online.

Books by Helene Gadot:

KINDRED SOULS SERIES:

Her Assassins

Her Prince

Her Dragon

Her Kindreds - coming soon

ACES AND KNAVES SERIES:

Crash

Boom – coming soon

DREAMS AND MAGIC SERIES:

Wicked Fae- coming August 2018

KEEP READING FOR A SNEAK PEEK OF HER PRINCE...

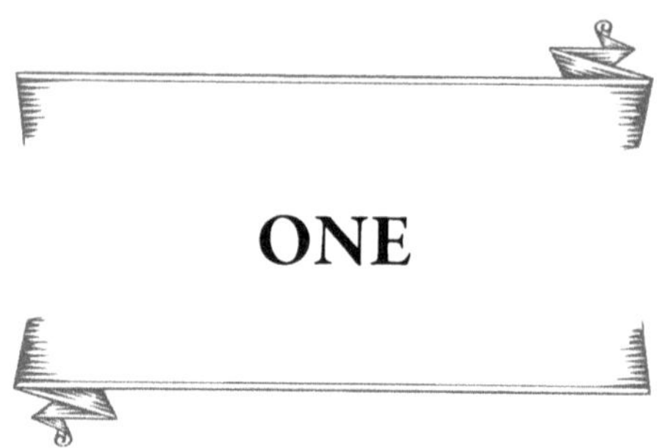

ONE

Morning sunlight streamed through the thin gray curtains as I plucked idly at the strings of my ukulele. Saber pressed kisses up my bare leg peeking from the pile of blankets.

My back arched when he reached my hip and I groaned. "Are you paying attention? You're supposed to be learning how to play. It was your idea."

"It was. But you're making it incredibly hard to focus." He inched the blanket over the slightest bit, uncovering my core and nibbled at my pelvis.

An embarrassing whimpering sound squeaked from my lips and my fingers jerked from my instrument with a screech. Limp fingers lost their grip on my ukulele as Saber unwrapped me completely, slowly, seductively, heat in his gaze as he looked up and down my naked and trembling body.

It'd been weeks, and I still wanted them. With a near constant ache. I thought the bond would relax once I gave in, but instead it still rode me, raging through me, keeping me in a constant state of need.

At least, I thought it was the bond.

I reached out and cupped Saber's cheek, enjoying the scratchy feeling of his new beard. He started growing it out over the past week though it was nowhere near as thick as Whist's. Saber looked good scruffy.

He smiled at me, the light in his eyes so bright it almost hurt. I couldn't stop the answering smile if I tried. For the first time in my life, I was safe, I was happy. The itch in my feet keeping me always on the move was gone. I hoped it lasted. I hoped the ghosts from my parents didn't return with disappointment and condemnation.

Over a week ago, I had laid their memory to rest when I made the choice to stay with my kindred souls. A choice I didn't regret, and one my parents would understand. But there was a small, tiny, minuscule part of me. A part of me I ignored. A part I drowned with the touch, taste, scent of my kindreds.

Only satiated and curled up between my sleeping assassins did the tiny voice gain any traction. It reminded me of my beliefs, it reminded me I wasn't really safe and wouldn't be with the king after us. It reminded me the law was still broken and wrong. And it reminded me of all the things my guys gave up for me. And what I gave up for them.

"Where are you, love?" Saber asked as he spread my legs.

I blinked away my thoughts. "Right here. I'm right here with you."

"Good."

"Aren't we supposed to leave soon?" I asked.

Saber and I lingered in bed while Sky and Whist went to make sure there weren't any royal guards in the area. Everything was packed and ready for our journey to Havisam. We had decided a couple days ago it was better for the four of us to start fresh, start a new life, instead of constantly living on the run here in Faligrey.

"We are. But we should have a little time."

I grinned. "Good."

Saber covered my body with his, teasing my mouth with a languid kiss. I opened my legs wider so he could settle more firmly against me, his steel cock nudging my entrance. My hands trailed up and down his smooth back as I deepened the kiss.

He groaned into my mouth, his hands wandering over my body. "You're beautiful, love. So responsive, so sweet, so delicious. I can't get enough of you. It's never enough."

I whimpered as he latched his mouth onto one of my nipples, writhing beneath him. At least I wasn't the only one out of control with want and desire. I wrapped my legs around his waist, tilting my hips to line us up. His tongue flirted with mine as he teased me by sinking just the tip of his cock inside me and circling his hips.

I wriggled to get him deeper inside, but he resisted with a chuckle. "What's the rush, love? I want to enjoy you."

"Because we're supposed to be getting ready to go and I don't want to be interrupted."

"They won't interrupt, they'll join."

"But we need to get on the road once they return."

He pressed in a little further. "Trust me, love. They won't mind getting a late start for this."

I groaned and tossed my head back into the pillows. They always did this, made me desperate for them before giving me what I craved, what I needed. If it didn't feel so damn amazing, it would've made me hate them.

Saber licked the side of my neck, sucking the skin at the base into his mouth. My nails sank into his back as I tried to get closer to him, wanting every inch of him against me, over me, in me.

Finally, finally, finally, he slammed home. We both let out harsh breaths, and he pulled back to gaze into my eyes. I couldn't look away from his eyes as he pumped in and out of me. We weren't fucking this time, filled with desperation and need. The desperation and need were still there, but muted. This time, it was something else, something deeper. Staring into his eyes, it was almost like I could see inside of him and he could see inside of me. We connected on a new level. The bond flared to life between us and I could almost read his thoughts. There were flashes of his emotions—affection, desire, friendship, attraction, admiration, awe, love. The love was tentative and new, but it grew stronger with each stroke.

We came together, gasping and shuddering, our gazes still locked together, our bodies one. He remained inside me even after we both caught our breath and our bodies had calmed.

He kissed the center of my forehead and slid out of me with reluctance.

I felt the same reluctance, fighting not to hold him tight. I wanted to bask in the afterglow, but the morning was growing late and we needed to get plenty of miles between us and this house today.

Like my thoughts alone summoned them, Sky and Whist burst in before Saber and I were even off the bed. Sky grinned wide while Whist leaned against the doorway and looked his fill.

"I thought you were teaching Saber how to play the ukulele?"

I blinked in utter innocence. "I was."

Sky's eyes danced with amused lights. "Perhaps he can give us a demonstration of all he learned."

I scoffed and pulled on my trousers. "We certainly don't have time for that."

Sky's lips pursed in an adorable pout. "Fine. It'll give us something to look forward to once we set up camp tonight."

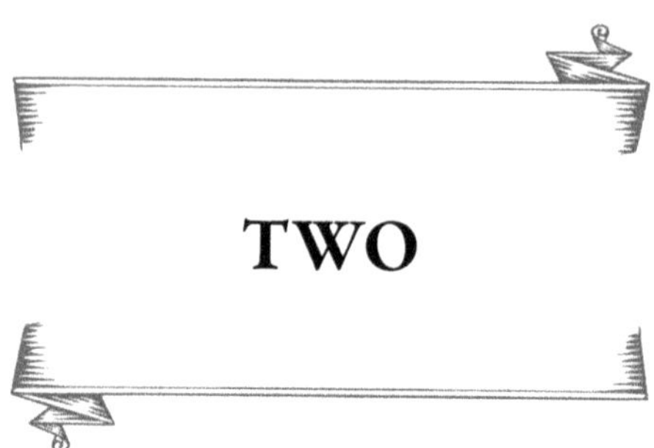

TWO

Sky insisted it was his turn with me, so I ended up basically in his lap on the back of the horse. He was worse than Whist with his teasing touches and whispered dirty words.

We were on the way to a new country. My breath caught and my stomach rolled.

It was scary, but exciting at the same time. No longer living a life constantly on the move, finally able to have a home, put down roots, create a family. I was sure Havisam had some laws I could protest against.

We hadn't discussed what our new lives would be like yet; the assassins said we'd figure it out. They had enough money squirreled away to get us set up. It burned not being able to contribute. Once we arrived, I'd find a way. I certainly would not sit back and let them take care of me.

"You still haven't told me much about your past."

Sky jerked at my words. We'd been riding in silence for a while. "What do you want to know?"

"Who are you leaving behind?" The guilt refused to let go, popping up over and over again.

His arms tightened around my middle. "Still worrying about this, doll?"

"Of course I am. You have to leave the country because of me."

"Not because of you. Because of the king. The only one leaving anyone behind who matters is Whist. And we'll figure out a way to get her out of there."

"Won't the king use her against him?" I asked.

Sky's fingers tripped down my thigh. "We told you, she's a favorite of the princesses and the prince. She'll be safe until we can smuggle her to Havisam."

"What about you and Saber's families?"

"We don't have any." His usual merry tone was flat and hard.

My stomach lurched. "What happened?"

"Saber's parents died when he was young and I was given to the orphanage as soon as I was born. It's how we met. We decided to become soldiers so we could stay together."

My brows furrowed and my heart hurt for the both of them. "Why haven't I heard this before?"

"Because it's depressing as fuck and we've been a bit busy the last couple weeks." He chuckled in my ear and slid his hand under my shirt.

But I wanted to get to know more than their bodies. I wanted to know them. I wanted them to know me.

We had given up everything for each other and I felt like we'd barely scratched the surface.

Sky nipped my ear. "What's going on in that head of yours, doll?"

"I just feel like we don't know each other very well." My eyes focused on Saber and Whist's backs as they rode in front of us, occasionally exchanging quiet words too low for me to hear.

"Little late for second thoughts." He pushed my hair over my shoulder to tease the back of my neck with his lips.

I shook my head and patted his leg. "Not second thoughts. I just want to know you."

"You will, doll. It takes time. We don't have to force it."

"You sound like Saber." I leaned back against him, my head in the crook of his neck.

"I hear that a lot. And you haven't told us much about your past either, you know. We know your parents weren't kindreds. We know you moved around your entire life. We know you spent the last few years traveling around as a bard making an enemy of the king. And that's about it."

"Fair enough." I pursed my lips.

"Let's get somewhere safe and settled. We'll have time for it. And we do know some things about you. Things like how brave you are, how strong, how stubborn, how fierce, how talented, how beautiful. And you know some things about us. Like how handsome and dashing and mysterious we are."

I snorted. But he wasn't wrong. I did know enough about them to know they were good men, dangerous men, my men. I knew they fit me like a missing puzzle piece, I knew they brought out sides of me I didn't know I had, I knew I was falling for them.

Sky was right. We had time. Determined to turn my mind off, I snuggled back into Sky's chest. He pressed a kiss onto the top of my head, making me smile.

Right as I began to nod off safe in his arms, our horse whinnied and reared. Sky kept me from falling and yanked the horse to a stop. He tossed me to the ground into Saber's arms before leaping to the ground and drawing his sword. Saber set me on my feet and shoved me behind him.

We were surrounded by royal guards.

www.ingramcontent.com/pod-product-compliance
Ingram Content Group UK Ltd.
Pitfield, Milton Keynes, MK11 3LW, UK
UKHW021934200726
13853UKWH00011B/1508

9 798407 114925